JUST
LET ME
LOVE
YOU

JUST LET ME LOVE YOU

S.R. GREY

Just Let Me Love You (Judge Me Not #3)
Copyright © 2014 by S.R. Grey

ISBN-10: 0692320415
ISBN-13: 978-0692320419

Editing: Hot Tree Editing
Cover Design: Arijana Karčić, Cover It! Designs
Interior Design and Formatting by: Tianne Samson with E.M. Tippetts Book Designs

BOOKS BY S.R. GREY

Judge Me Not

I Stand Before You
Never Doubt Me
Just Let Me Love You

The Harbour Falls Mysteries

Harbour Falls
Willow Point
Wickingham Way

Inevitability

Inevitable Detour
Inevitable Circumstances

I stand before you
Judge me not
Never doubt me
Judge me not
Just let me love you
Judge me not

PROLOGUE

Kay

C HASE comes down the steps a few minutes following my angry departure from the bedroom. I'm still pissed at him, which is why I'm standing at the front door contemplating whether I should leave.

My ire lets up a bit, though, when I see the suitcase in his hand. *This is really happening.* Leaning back against the wall by the door, my eyes can't meet his. Chase is truly doing this. He's leaving without me by his side.

I'm still a little surprised he kept secrets from me, but the initial sting has subsided. I knew he was holding stuff back. I didn't press; I just allowed myself to believe he had his reasons. It's my fault as much as it is his that he kept stuff buried. I should have made him fess up sooner.

But it doesn't really matter, not anymore. I know the truth now. Or rather, I know what he wants me to *think* is the truth. I know Chase, though, and there's no way those wounds on his hand were caused from hitting a person. He hit something inanimate that night; of that, I have no doubt. As for what happened with Doug, all I know is that whatever Chase did, it kept my ex away from me. That makes his actions justified in my eyes. Plus, how can I be angry? I did nothing to discourage him from seeking out my ex-boyfriend. Truthfully, I knew in my heart the day I told Chase of Doug's intentions to apologize to me that he would take action.

And he did. So I am as culpable as he.

I have to admit, though, when Chase arched his eyebrow at me, questioningly, at the mention of our engagement, I was shocked and hurt. And I'm still bristling. I mean, what the hell did that arched eyebrow mean? That we're not really engaged, or that being engaged means nothing?

Chase nears where I'm standing and sets his suitcase on the floor. I glance his way. His eyes hold a million apologies but I know no matter how sorry he feels, he is not going to bend. He's not going to take me to Las Vegas with him.

I glance away, and he says softly, "Kay."

I don't respond, but he's not deterred. He comes to me and wraps his strong arms around me.

"Don't," I snap, twisting away.

"Come on, baby girl," he soothes. "Don't leave it like this."

I resist meeting his blues, but his fingers find my chin and I have no choice but to look up at him.

His eyes hold nothing but truth, sincerity, and remorse. "I'm sorry, Kay," he says. "I'm sorry I kept secrets. I'm sorry I hurt you."

I cave a little. "Did you really beat the junkie?"

"What do you think?" he asks.

"No."

"And Doug?"

"Just talked to him."

"I wouldn't have cared if you beat him," I say, "not for his sake. But I'm glad you didn't, for yours."

Chase sighs, lowering his hand from my chin. "I don't want to fight anymore, Kay. I'm sorry I mocked our engagement that way. It was shitty. But you know I love you, right? And, if you'll still have me, I still want to get married."

"We could get married in Vegas," I say slyly.

"Kay..." Chase sighs. "I have to do this alone. You can't come to Vegas, not under these circumstances."

There's hesitation in his voice now, hesitation that wasn't there when we were arguing upstairs. Maybe Chase is second-guessing his decision to leave me behind. Damn, he knows we're better together than we are apart. And he can keep me safe in Vegas, just like I'll keep him grounded.

But before I can say any of this, Chase mutters, "I'd better go."

There's a short good-bye kiss, a long hug, and then he's gone. I can't bring myself to watch him drive away. It hurts too much.

After he's gone, I aimlessly walk around downstairs, from room to room. But the emptiness of the house without Chase in it is too much to handle. I head up to the bedroom, where everything still smells like my guy — fresh, soapy, male.

There's an indentation on the bed where the suitcase was. I erase the reminder that Chase is gone by reaching down and smoothing out the covers. Suddenly, I feel exhausted. I lie down on the bed and press my nose to Chase's pillow, whispering his name.

Rolling to my back, I stare up at the wall. Above me hangs the oil pastel of the Eiffel Tower, the sketch Chase drew for me not so very long ago. The drawing is beautiful, and I can't help but smile when I recall the many times Chase and I have talked, laughed, and loved beneath this little piece of Paris.

Paris…

I'm reminded of the evening Chase brought Paris to me, the night of our rooftop picnic at sunset. Everything was so perfect. We feasted on brie spread over pieces of baguette; we drank pink-tinged Kir that matched the sunset that evening. But, best of all, Chase and I made love for the first time that night.

Chase gave me a memory, a beautiful memory, to hold close to my heart. I knew even then that that memory would soothe me in troubled times such as these.

And it does; that memory soothes me now.

My head starts to clear and I get a hold of any lingering wayward emotions. *Time to quit lying around, time to quit moping – it's time to take action.*

But I'm not exactly sure what I should do.

Rising up to my knees, I glance around.

My cell is on the nightstand. Usually I handle things by myself, or with Chase, but maybe if I talk with someone else, I'll find the direction I seek.

Heck, it's worth a try.

My first impulse is to call Father Maridale, since he's generally a help when I feel uncertain, but I hesitate. Tonight, I feel speaking with a woman might be more helpful to me.

Decided and determined, I reach out and grab my cell from the nightstand. But then I just stare blankly at it. Who can I call—Missy? No, she's dealing with her own things. Sadly, I don't really have any other female friends.

To be honest, I know who I'd *like* to speak with.

But I am hesitant to call her.

"Oh, what the hell," I say out loud, resolving to do the one thing I never would have imagined myself doing even just a month ago.

I call my mother.

In some inexplicable, weird way it feels right, like my mother and I have progressed to this point, and it's my turn to reach out. As Father Maridale counseled, I am giving her an opportunity to be here for me. My mother has initiated all contact up to this point; she always calls me. She's been great so far, too; keeping up with me, warning me about Doug. But this will mark the first time I've taken it upon myself to get in touch with her.

I breathe in deeply. *Let's see how this goes...*

To my delight, when I reach her, my mom sounds genuinely pleased to hear from me. That kind of response touches me deep inside. This is the connection I've longed for ever since Mom turned away. Before then, even. I always wanted a real relationship with my mother. After all, she is my flesh and blood and there's a bond there that transcends hurt feelings and past wrongs, no matter how deeply they run.

We talk, just small talk. I keep the conversation light, updating her on what we've been doing, like the fair Chase and I took Will and Jared to, our road trip to Pittsburgh, movies we've seen, that sort of thing.

At one point, Mom asks me how work is going, and I reply, "Actually, I'm pretty much done with the secretary gig. That was just for the summer."

"School doesn't start till September, though," she remarks.

"That's true," I reply, "but the regular secretary, Connie, returns on Monday from her trip. She and her husband were on an extended cruise."

"Oh, so you have the next three weeks off?"

"Yeah," I confirm. "Father Maridale told me I can still come in and help Connie if I get bored, but there's really no need. I'm sure I'll find plenty of things to do around here."

There's a smile in Mom's voice as she states, "Look on the bright side, honey. Think of how much time you and Chase can spend together these next few weeks. You have the rest of August to do things before you go back to teaching. These dog days of summer are so nice for young couples; lots of end-of-summer events and activities to enjoy."

"Um..."

Mom, misunderstanding my non-reply, says, "Oh, what am I going on about? I'm sure Chase still has to work the rest of the month. Just never mind me, honey."

Chase would still be working through August, but when Father Maridale was told of the latest troubles with Will, he gave Chase the rest of the month off.

Damn. Mom's words resonate, and I think of how I'd love to be planning fun, end-of-summer activities for Chase and me to partake in. But who knows how much of the next few weeks we'll even end up spending together. Chase might be stuck in Vegas for a while.

When I don't immediately respond to my mom, she says, as only moms can do, "Kay, what's wrong?"

I need to talk to someone and she really is trying, so I confess to her that Chase is gone. "He's on his way to the airport right now. Chase is flying out to Las Vegas early tomorrow morning to, uh, help his brother. I don't know how long he'll be gone."

Mom sighs, then says with much kindness, "I'm sorry, Kay."

That prompts me to spill everything that has really been happening. Well, almost everything. I leave out my argument with Chase, and I don't dare mention that Will purchased a gun. I do, however, share with my mother that a misguided Will might run into trouble while trying to protect his girlfriend.

My mom is quiet for a few beats, like maybe she's assessing. Sure enough, she says softly, "You want to go with Chase, don't you?"

"I do," I admit. Why lie?

"So, why aren't you with him now?" she gently prods.

I stifle a sniffle. "He wants to do this alone, Mom. He thinks I'll get caught up in what he terms *a dangerous situation*." I sigh. "This thing with Will, it's, uh, volatile. Besides, Chase told me he needs to do this on his own."

Even though my responses are vague, I expect my mother to do what she's always done—start up with her judgments.

But she does nothing of the sort. Instead of blurting out something cutting or biting, she says, "Honey, don't ever doubt yourself. And don't let Chase doubt you, either. It sounds to me like he might need you with him more than he realizes."

I consider her words and mumble a "maybe."

"Kay," she continues, "sometimes men underestimate what we, as women, can handle. Chase wants to protect you, sure, and that's noble, but maybe he needs you to show him what you're made of. Show him the strong woman I know you are, honey. Show him how *your* strength can actually strengthen *him*."

"He knows I'm strong," I reply softly. "I mean, I think he does."

"*Show* him you are," Mom responds.

"How?" I whisper.

Her answer is simple, but powerful. "Go to him, Kay."

Sage advice from a woman I thought had given up on me, a woman I almost gave up on myself. I feel elated that I've made this call; it was absolutely the right thing to do.

And since I'm ready to keep making better decisions, I announce, "I *am* going to go to him. I'll book a ticket and pack as soon as we finish up here."

I hear a smile in Mom's voice as she says, "Then I'd better let you go, sweetie."

"Okay."

But before we disconnect, my mother adds, "Be safe, Kay. And if there's anything you need, anything at all, just call me, okay?"

"I will," I promise, and then I say, "Oh, and Mom…"

"Yes?"

"Thank you."

Two hours later, I am on the turnpike, heading out of Ohio and into Pennsylvania. Another twenty minutes and I should be arriving at the airport in Pittsburgh. Surely, my presence will surprise the hell out of Chase. I expect he may resist the idea of me going with him at first, like he did back at the house, but I am *not* changing my mind. No matter what he says or does.

Nope, I am going to Las Vegas with Chase Gartner. I'm booked on the same flight, and I was even able to book the seat next to him.

There's no going back now.

"Never doubt me," I whisper to myself as I drive.

It's what I'd say to Chase if he were here, because what he doesn't realize is that danger doesn't frighten me. I've faced a lot, and I've come through everything okay. Maybe a little roughed up sometimes, yes, but I've kept going.

Besides, when it comes right down to it, I'd walk into the fires of Hell for Chase. I love him that much, though I don't think things will come to *that*.

The situation with Chase's brother is bound to be resolved. I just hope it's in a way in which everyone comes out safe.

But no matter what happens, one thing is certain: Chase and I are going to overcome this obstacle in the same way we've faced everything else—together.

ONE

Chase

"CHASE, wake up. I'm here."
A female voice, I know that voice.
Wait, I *love* the person that voice belongs to.
"Kay," I whisper.

"Yes, it's me." She shakes my shoulder then tries—unsuccessfully, I might add—to lift me from where I'm lying on my back in a corner area of boarding gate B17. It's not the most comfortable spot to sleep—scratchy carpeting, no pillow—but when you're exhausted you make do.

"I'm here," the voice continues. "Wake up, baby."

Kay, the love of my life, is here at the airport in Pittsburgh. I can't believe it. My forgiving girl, she didn't let the harsh words I spewed before I left the farmhouse—back where we live in Ohio—stop her. Sure, we kind of worked things out before I took off, but I have no doubt she was still all kinds of pissed at me.

Maybe she's not so very angry, after all, seeing as she's here with me, saying my name...again.

Relief floods me. Kay doesn't sound angry at all. She sounds forgiving and beautiful.

Even so, I roll to my side and drift back to sleep. Kay is beauty, forgiveness, and love, but sleep offers blissful oblivion. And with what I'm about to embark on, I need a few more minutes of oblivion.

I drift back to where I was before Kay arrived — dreaming. In this dream, I am fourteen years old again, living in a beautiful, contemporary home. I know the house well. It's the house my parents once owned, before we fell into financial ruin. And before my dad decided to drive off a cliff in the Nevada desert, ending his time on this planet.

Yeah, before *those* things happened.

My mom is happy in this dreamland of mine, having not yet discovered the lure of gambling, and my little brother Will is just that — little. He hasn't yet learned of drugs and how they can make him feel. He's bright-eyed and clear-headed. More importantly, the guns he plays with aren't real; they are only toys.

Also in Dreamland, Will doesn't have a girlfriend he feels the need to save. And that is a blessing I wish were real.

"Cassie," I murmur, annoyed.

An image of Will's ethereal-looking girlfriend infiltrates my good dream, turning it sour. Cassie may look like some waif-like, golden-haired angel, but she's far from pure. In my opinion, she's no good for Will. She's as mixed-up and confused as my brother, which does him no good. Worse yet, Cassie is surrounded by devils. After all, it is her fucked-up stepdad, Paul, who has given Will a reason to return early to Vegas.

Will was staying with me for the summer until he

learned of Paul's latest misconduct toward Cassie. Yeah, finding out that Paul had his hands on his sixteen-year-old girlfriend—albeit only briefly—was more than enough motivation to put that kid on a bus heading west.

A bus I hope to catch up to sometime tomorrow.

Hence the airport I'm lying in, dreaming; hence the flight I've booked to Vegas. If I don't intercept Will, disaster could ensue. Because, shit, Lord only knows what little bro has planned. Unfortunately, I suspect it's something that involves a gun. And with the right combination of fury and drugs, my brother could very well decide there's a bullet in the chamber of that very gun with Paul's name on it.

Fuck.

I shudder, and Kay shakes me again. "Come on, Chase," she says, irritated. "No one can sleep this soundly. Wake up."

She's aggravated, but her small hands feel so good on me. I'm reminded that Dreamland is illusory—things can change on a dime. But Kay, my Kay, offers real comfort.

I open my eyes and peer up at her porcelain face, her chestnut mane of hair flowing down her shoulders in waves.

I murmur what I'm thinking, "Beautiful."

"Chase," she says, sighing.

My eyes meet her caramel-colored gaze, and I mumble a sleepy, "Hey."

"Hey, back at you," she replies with a smile that warms me to no end.

"You came," I croak out, my voice thick from sleep.

"Did you really think you could keep me away?" Kay asks. But then she pauses, contemplates, and adds, "Wait. Don't answer that."

"I'm a fool," I say, reaching up and touching her face. "I should've known better."

She covers my hand with hers. "You were only trying to protect me. I know that now."

After giving her cheek a light caress—I always want to touch her—I drop my hand to my side. Sitting up, I rake my fingers through my hair. Glancing around the boarding area, I sigh. I'm thankful that it's empty.

"Yeah," I murmur, shaking the last cobwebs of sleep from my head. "I always want to keep you safe, true, but it seems I have a knack for going about it in the absolute worst way."

This is so true; our relationship is littered with my mistakes.

Kay scoots closer, and now it's she who is touching me...my hand, my arm.

She leans in and kisses my cheek. "You don't go about it in the worst way," she whispers. "Not at all, Chase."

"Still, you're better at this shit than me."

Scoffing, she says, "Ha, I am far from perfect. We're learning this stuff together, remember?"

"What stuff?" I turn, facing her more fully. "Learning how to be in love, or learning how to be in a relationship?"

"Both," she says. "All of it."

"Come here."

I wrap my arms around her and maneuver our bodies till she's seated in my lap. "All I know, Kay, is that I love you so much," I whisper in her hair.

"I love you, too," she replies, her lips full of promise as they travel down my neck.

I'd like to stay like this forever—wrapped up together, wrapped up in love—but a damn gate agent arrives and spoils the moment.

When she glances over at us and frowns, I say, "Shit," as I slide Kay off my lap.

"What's wrong?" Kay asks as she tucks her legs under her and smoothes the hem of her dress.

I jerk my head to the agent. "We're not alone anymore. And I don't think she's in the mood for putting up with our public displays of affection."

"Oh." Kay's brow creases with disappointment when she glances over at the less-than-happy agent. "Yeah, I guess we should probably get up off the floor and sit in the seats like normal people."

I don't know how normal we are, but I agree, "Yeah, we should probably move."

The boarding area is still devoid of other passengers, but Kay and I opt for sitting as far away from the gate and the displeased agent as possible.

A few minutes after we're settled, other passengers begin to filter in.

As I watch a line form at the counter, I remember something important. Nudging Kay, I say, "Hey, we should probably get in line, don't you think?"

"Why?" Kay asks, confused.

"Well, we need to buy you a ticket if you're definitely coming to Las Vegas with me."

"Oh, I'm definitely coming with you, Chase," she assures me, all determined, like she's afraid I'm going to change my mind and try to send her back to Ohio.

As if that action would ever be possible with this stubborn woman.

I laugh a little at the resolute expression on Kay's adorable face, and then, rising to my feet, I offer her my hand. "Okay, Miss Determined, let's go buy you a ticket, then."

Kay doesn't budge. Softly, she says, "Um, I already took care of that."

"You already have a ticket?"

"Yes," she replies sheepishly.

I give her a look, a not-happy look. "Kay, please don't tell me you used your emergency credit card."

"Um, well…" She glances away. "Okay, yeah, I did use my emergency card."

With my grandmother's property and savings I inherited, I'm financially better off than Kay, so I say, "I hope you know I'm paying that bill when it comes in."

My tone is pretty damn insistent, and Kay nods an assent.

And then, since I'm curious, I ask, "What made you decide to buy a ticket, anyway? I mean, I knew you wanted to come with me, but when I was leaving you looked pretty much resigned with staying in Harmony Creek."

"I was planning on staying," she admits.

"So, what happened?"

She laughs and says, "You wouldn't believe it if I told you."

"Try me," I reply, raising a brow.

Shit, truth is, I'm now more curious than ever. What could have convinced Kay to take such a definitive measure?

I can't imagine, but she just about floors me when she says, "I talked with my mother and she convinced me to buy the ticket and go with you to Nevada."

"You're kidding," I reply dryly.

Yeah, I'm not the biggest fan of Kay's mom. And why should I be? Mrs. Stanton abandoned Kay when the youngest in the family, Sarah, died in a tragic way. She blamed Kay for years for something I saw in, like, two seconds was an accident, after hearing the whole story. In any case, Kay's mother has only recently made a return to her life. I suppose the woman is sincere, but I can't help but feel wary.

"Yeah," Kay replies, oblivious to my unspoken misgivings. "My mom said that sometimes men don't realize how strong their women are. She said you, for example, might need a little reminding."

Kay gives me a withering look, one that makes me laugh and pull her to me. "Oh, she said that, did she?" I kiss Kay's cheek. "Don't worry, baby. I know you're strong."

She leans away, her eyes meeting mine. "Do you, Chase? I mean, do you really think I'm strong?"

"I'm more certain of your strength than your mother is. I have no doubt about that."

Kay frowns, and I add, "Hey, I know you're strong because you ground me. You give me stability, Kay Stanton. You make me right. And trust me...that is no small feat."

I don't add that I have about a dozen reservations. Not about her, God no. And not about our relationship, either. My reservations are about one thing only—me.

Truth is I don't know if I'm all that great for Kay. My insecurities and fears run so fucking deep, all the way down to my tarnished, repentant soul. I spent years burying all my unresolved garbage with shit like drugs, fighting, fucking anything that moved. Great guy, huh?

Four years in prison straightened me out in many ways, but I've been known to relapse from time to time. Safe to say, I am far from healed.

As if she senses what I might be thinking, Kay touches the side of my head, her fingers weaving in my hair. "Chase, what's going on in there?" she asks.

The gate agent suddenly announces that our red-eye flight is boarding, putting an end to a potentially uncomfortable discussion. *Thank God.*

Standing, I offer my hand to Kay. "Let's go, babe," I say. "Let's go save my brother."

TWO

Kay

Las Vegas is hot. No, it's scorching.

"August is obviously not a good month to come to the desert." I press some buttons and lower all the windows in the sensible white sedan Chase and I have rented.

Hot air wafts in, and I mumble under my breath, "That's not much better."

"No," Chase says. "August is far from the ideal time of the year to visit this place."

We're still in the rental lot, and Chase starts the car. The air-conditioner blows out a noisy stream of semi-cool air, and it slowly becomes more comfortable in time. Enough so that I'm able to close the windows by the time we're leaving the airport.

Ten minutes later, it's positively frosty in the car. "Brrr," I say, shivering.

I turn down the air, and Chase laughs. "Too cold now?"

Wrapping my arms around myself, I say, "Yeah, a little."

"We could turn off the air and open the windows. You'll warm up again in no time."

"No," I reply. "I'm good."

As Chase and I drive up the famous Las Vegas Strip, I soon forget all about being cold. There are too many distractions, too many things to see.

"Wow," I murmur as I try to take in everything at once.

There's a shiny, mirrored-glass pyramid, and next to that crazy structure is something that looks like a fairyland castle. A few minutes more and we are passing a hotel with dancing fountains, and then there's a resort with a big pirate ship out in the front.

"I feel like I'm in some crazy wonderland," I say to Chase.

I turn to him, all wide-eyed and excited, and he harrumphs. "I don't know about the wonderland part, but this place is definitely crazy."

My excitement is tempered as I remember that this place is nothing special to Chase. Glancing over at him, sneakily so he doesn't notice, I try to assess how he's holding up. He is gorgeous, as always, but he appears worried and exhausted, as well. Still, how this man can pull off beautiful and sexy with hardly any sleep the previous night is anyone's guess. But the facts are the facts, and in a tight navy-blue T-shirt that accentuates his muscular arms and faded jeans—a rip at one knee—Chase accomplishes exactly that. He truly is male perfection.

How did I get so lucky? I muse.

Smiling, I place a hand on the knee with the rip. "Are you thinking about Will?" I gently ask.

"I am," Chase replies.

"And...?" I prompt.

I know there's more. Something is bothering him.

Glancing at the clock in the dash, Chase blows out a breath and says, "I think we've probably missed him at the bus station."

Will's bus was due in fifteen minutes ago, so Chase is surely right. Damn. I knew from the start we'd be cutting it close — racing against the clock — and, sadly, it looks like we lost this battle.

Chase needs reassurance right now, though, so I say encouragingly, "We'll find Will. Nothing bad will happen."

Convincing, that's the tone I'm striving for. And I succeed — I sound so very convincing. Too bad what I'm really feeling is about ten pounds of worry on my shoulders. That worry quickly increases to twenty pounds when we make it to the bus station and, sure enough, the bus Will came in on has come and gone.

"Will's gone," Chase says dejectedly as he drops down into a hard plastic chair bolted down to the floor of the stuffy bus station lounge.

It's noisy and uncomfortable in the crusty, old terminal. I sit down next to Chase and place my head on his shoulder. I'm pretty well spent myself.

After a minute of shared respite, I lift my head. "It's been a long night and a long morning, Chase. Let's drive up to your mom's house. Who knows, maybe Will is home."

Chase doesn't reply, and when I look over at him he raises an eyebrow. His eyes, eyes I long ago christened gunmetal-blue, appear tired, clouded with worry.

"And if he's not there?" he asks. "Then what do we do, Kay?"

"Well, we can get some sleep and maybe something to eat. We'll go out afterward and look for Will. We'll stay out all night if we have to, but we need to re-charge."

Again, I try so hard to sound confident and sure. Of

course, the truth is I know nothing more than what Chase knows. And that is next to nothing. Will could literally be anywhere by now. Still, starting at the house he lives in seems like a reasonable plan.

Chase has never been to the house his mother shares with her new husband Greg, and Will, but he knows the address. Back in the rental car, he sets the GPS accordingly.

And then we're on our way.

A short while later, outside a gated community of affluent homes, the neighborhood where Abby and Greg live, Chase slows down considerably. Muttering, "Jesus," he blows out a breath.

"Wow," is my only response as we make our way through the ritzy plan of homes.

"Mom really did hit the jackpot when she married Greg," Chase says, shaking his head.

"You're not kidding," I mumble.

The houses—no, *mansions*—are nothing short of spectacular. Following the GPS instructions, we wind through the palm tree-lined streets. We soon discover the house the former Abby Gartner lives in is tucked away behind an elaborate garden of cacti and desert flora.

There's a large, black wrought-iron gate at the entrance to her home, and even though the gate is open, we stop. Ironically, the open gate is askew, making it look unnervingly similar to the much smaller wrought-iron gate that marks the entrance to the cemetery behind the church where Chase and I work.

I suspect Chase notices this too. I'm soon sure he notices when I catch him staring at the gate for a longer-than-necessary amount of time before driving through.

"Remind you of something?" he quietly asks.

"That gate looks like the one at the cemetery behind Holy Trinity."

Chase chuckles humorlessly. "Yeah, it sure does. And

it's pretty fucking weird."

"Very," I reply.

The similarity is weird on a number of levels. But I'm too tired to dwell on the symbolism of how the entrance to Chase's mom's house matches the entrance to a place where the dead rest.

Chase drives forward, following the curve of the driveway until we reach the front of the house.

After we park and step out of the car, I realize something. "Wait, you don't have a key, Chase. How are we supposed to get in the house?"

So far, access hasn't been a problem. The gates at the entrance to the neighborhood were open. Same with the weird Holy Trinity-duplicate gate here at the house. But I have no doubt the house itself will be secured. Abby and Greg have been on a cruise for the past couple of weeks, and Will has been with Chase and me in Ohio. I doubt the place has been unlocked all this time.

Despite my concerns, not having a key turns out not to be a problem.

As Chase and I walk tentatively up to a wide set of steps leading to the house, the front door swings open.

Chase and I skid to a stop, and there is Will, standing before us.

When he sees us—like, *really* sees we are truly there—his green eyes widen. "Holy shit, what the fuck are you two doing here?" he exclaims.

Chase dispenses with any form of greeting and gets right to the point. "I know everything, Will. Jared came to see me yesterday afternoon. So, I think you know why we are here."

"Oh, shit," Will mutters.

"*Oh, shit* is right," Chase snaps as he takes a step in Will's direction. "I want that gun, bro."

"I don't know what you're talking about."

Will tries to sound smooth, noncommittal, but his eyes betray him. He looks guilty, guilty, guilty.

"Jared told us *everything*," I interject. "We know you bought a gun from Kyle Tanner."

Will knows he's busted, so he tries a different tact. "So what if I did? Having a gun is no big deal. It's dangerous out here in Sin City. I need something to protect myself with."

"Protect yourself...or protect Cassie?" Chase tosses out accusingly.

"Uh..." Will can't maintain eye contact with his brother.

He glances away, and Chase blows out a frustrated breath. "Look," he says, gesturing to the front door Will is standing in front of. "Let's talk about this inside, okay?"

When Will doesn't budge, Chase walks forward and pushes past him, barging right into the house.

Will leans back on the doorjamb and groans, "Dude, really?"

When I walk past Will, following Chase, I give him a disappointed look. He just rolls his eyes.

I rush to catch up with Chase, but when he stops abruptly I almost wreck right into his broad back and shoulders.

"Why did you stop...?" I start to ask. But the words die on my lips.

Wow.

I need no explanation as I scan our surroundings. The opulence of the interior of the house is enough to make anyone stop in their tracks. Standing next to Chase in the center of a huge entry hall, I take it all in—the soaring spiral staircase to my right, the sparkling crystal chandelier overhead, and the beautifully colored marble everywhere.

"Fuck," Chase mutters as he slowly turns in a circle.

I glance back at the doorway. Will looks pleased as can

be that this ostentatious house has distracted Chase from his original intention.

Hurrying over to stand next to Chase, Will says, "Pretty sweet, right?"

From the other side of Chase, I touch his forearm. "Are you okay?" I ask.

I'm concerned since he's not answering his brother's question.

But everything Chase isn't voicing is right there in his eyes — pain, sadness, awe, disbelief. Chase spent four years surrounded by and staring at cold prison walls. Walls made of concrete, walls that held nothing but what Chase could create with his own hands — his artwork.

I glance around at the no-doubt pricey paintings on these walls. Chase's art is still better, always will be in my eyes. I bet Abby doesn't even remember that her oldest son paints and draws like nobody's business.

And that is absolutely tragic.

Could she really forget that much of Chase?

Maybe, I conclude. Maybe, seeing as there's nothing in this house to indicate Abby has another son besides Will. It's sad, but maybe it's easier to forget that son. Maybe it's easier than thinking of how you sent him away, how your actions helped land him in prison.

Jack Gartner, Chase's deceased father, was no saint either.

The sins of the father were visited upon the once-prodigal son six years ago. After his father's suicide, Chase sought out drinking, drugs, fighting, and loose women. But he paid dearly for those vices. Chase was sent to prison for four years. And while he was left to suffer, his mother went on and rebuilt her life without him. She had already cast him aside when he was eighteen, sent him adrift with nothing. And this is where she ended up — living in this house.

Abby fought her own demons for a while—gambling and men—but what price did she pay? She paid nothing, as it seems she was rewarded in the end.

Life is sometimes not fair, not fair at all.

If I'm thinking all these things, how could Chase not be?

Certain that he is, I reach out and touch the stubble along his clenched jaw. Rubbing gently against the scruff, I ask, "Chase, are you all right?"

He places his hand over mine, lowering our clasped hands slowly. "I'm fine, Kay," he states flatly.

Will senses the tension, and it shows in his unsteady voice when he says, "Uh, so, if you guys are staying I can show you where the guest bedrooms are. You can choose whichever room you like. And you can take showers, too." He glances at our empty hands. "That is, if you remembered to bring some luggage."

"We brought luggage," Chase mutters distractedly. "It's in the trunk of the rental car."

"I'll go get it," Will offers helpfully.

Before anyone can reply, he is out the door.

"Hey"—I unclasp our hands and touch Chase's arm—"are you really okay?"

His eyes meet mine. "Yeah, I'm good, babe. It's just this house…" He shakes his head and blows out a breath.

"I know," I acknowledge. "I know."

Will returns with our suitcases in hand. He is all smiles now that Chase has been thrown off-course. But I know Chase will get back to interrogating Will. He'll find out where he is stowing that gun, and he'll get to the bottom of why Will bought the damn thing in the first place.

An hour later, Chase and I are showered and changed into jeans and tees. We're in a guest bedroom Chase picked out. It was the first one we came to, and Will couldn't believe he had chosen so quickly.

Confused, he said, "There are nicer rooms in the next hall over. You should check those out, bro."

"This one is good," Chase flatly said to his brother. "It'll do."

Will started to go, but then he spun around and offered to heat up macaroni and cheese he had made an hour earlier. Apparently, Will arrived just a short while before us, having taken a taxi from the bus station.

"Do you want to go down and eat?" I ask Chase.

He's lying on the bed, prone across a downy-white coverlet. I'm in front of the dresser, brushing out my hair. Chase's hair is a mess, still damp from his shower. He's in need of a trim, but I haven't said anything. He's far too sexy with his mess of light-brown locks.

Chase's eyes remain closed, even though I'm talking to him, but I know he's awake.

Sure enough, he opens one eye when I take a step closer to the bed. And then, a second later, I am on the bed, pinned under his hard, unyielding strength.

Chase's nose travels along my neck then down to my collarbone. "Now that you mention it," he murmurs. "I am kind of hungry."

"We should head down, then," I reply in a whisper as kisses me senseless.

He murmurs in my ear, "What I'm hungry for is right here." He shifts, letting me feel just what wants.

"Chase," I groan. "I'd love to, I would, but you know we don't have time. Will is waiting downstairs—"

My words are cut off by raw kisses that make me forget things like food, time, Will waiting downstairs.

In seconds, Chase has my jeans and panties off. He pushes up my tee, unclasping my bra. I'm almost fully exposed to him as he lowers his pants and boxer briefs just enough to free his erection.

Chase is fevered and hot, impatient in his need to have

me. He pushes my legs apart and plunges into me without prelude.

"Aah," I moan.

He moves in and out of me slowly, giving my body time to accommodate him.

And I do open for him. I grow wetter and wetter, and soon I am asking, "God, Chase, why do you always feel so good?"

Chase moves in me, pressing his body down on me. He wraps his arms around me and rasps, "It's you who always feels so good, Kay."

When he buries his face in my neck, I hear him almost indistinctly mumble, "I just wish I had more to give you."

He doesn't mean sex; I get a lot of that. In fact, I think Chase sometimes uses sex to avoid dealing with other issues—like the one obviously weighing on him today.

I tense, and he stops moving. "Hey, don't say that," I say into his hair. "You give me everything. You've given me my life back, Chase."

Before meeting Chase, I was not living. I merely existed, until Chase showed me how to laugh and how to have fun again. He gave me love, and in doing so he taught me how to forgive myself.

"Why do you keep saying things like that?" I ask.

Chase is not moving, but he's still inside me as he lifts his head and gazes down at me. "Because it's true," he says.

He pulls out of me and flops onto his back.

I roll to my side and reach for him, but I falter when he says, "Do you want to know why I think that? Why I say I wish I had more to give you so often?"

"Yes," I say. "I want to know."

Scrubbing his hand down his face, Chase says, "My heart belongs to you, Kay, all of it." He sighs. "But I don't know if that's enough."

"What do you mean?"

"My heart is all cut up, baby girl. Part of my heart died when my father died. And part of it is wrecked from my past."

My own heart aches at hearing his words. I can feel his pain, his deep regret.

"My heart's all parceled up, too," I remind him.

He looks over at me, sadness in his blues. "There's still more than enough for me," he tells me.

I place my hand on his chest, right where his heart beats below. "There's more than enough in here"—I tap his chest—"for me, too."

"What about Will?" Chase says, his chest rising and falling, his heart beating strong beats under my hand. "I feel like loving him so much has taken love away from you."

"Oh, Chase. You have it all wrong. Loving your brother has nothing to do with us."

He turns his head to face me, giving me a look like I'm joking.

"Really, Kay, do you truly believe that? Because the way I see it, if it weren't for this trouble with Will, you and I would be back in Harmony Creek right now. We'd be living and loving and enjoying all the shit we're missing out on by being here."

I try to find the bright spot in all of this. I want Chase to stop thinking in such a negative way.

"Will is here at the house," I say. "He's not out chasing Paul, like you thought he'd be. This will all be over soon and everything will be back to normal."

"I doubt it, Kay," Chase scoffs. "I know my brother, and this shit is far from done."

"But you're in Vegas now. You'll straighten him out."

I smile over at him, and he says sadly, "My sweet Kay, always believing in me."

If only Chase believed in himself half as much.

I crawl over and settle on top of him. He's not hard anymore, but that situation changes quickly when I reach down and place him at my slick core. "I'll always believe in you," I say.

I move, sliding down on his hardening length slowly.

"Why?" he asks, his breaths becoming more and more ragged, even as he resists the inevitable.

Leaning down, I brush my lips over his. "Because I love you...and you love me."

"Is it enough?" he asks, pained.

"It's going to have to be," I murmur.

I continue to slide up and down his shaft, my movements more and more insistent until Chase has no choice but to react as nature intended.

He thrusts up into me, his fingers digging into my hips.

And then there is no more talk; there's only the sound of our love, a love I can only hope will prove to be enough.

THREE

Chase

WILL eyes us suspiciously when Kay and I finally make it downstairs for our Mac-n-Cheese dinner. "Well, that took forever," he snaps.

I am not amused by his belligerent attitude and tell him to zip it as Kay and I sit down at the dining room table.

"Whatever, dude," he replies. "Like I don't know what you were doing. I swear, you two are like rabbits."

I shoot him a displeased look, but he hurries back in the direction of the kitchen. By the time he emerges, three steaming-hot plates of macaroni and cheese balanced precariously in his hands, my irritation dissipates. I just thank Will for the grub when he hands me my dish.

And then, as my brother places Kay's plate of cheesy macaroni in front of her, he announces, "By the way, guys, Cassie is coming over tonight to watch a movie."

Will takes a seat across from me and Kay, smiling smugly.

I shoot him a withering look. "Do you really think that's a good idea, Will? I wanted to talk to you about a few things." I take a bite of macaroni, and after I swallow and take a sip of water, I add, "Why don't you call Cassie and tell her you'll see her tomorrow."

Will snorts. "Yeah, right, dude. You and I can talk tomorrow. We're at Mom's house now, not yours. You're not in charge, and, around here, the rules are different."

"No shit," I murmur.

I've only been here a couple of hours and already Will is pushing my buttons. He knows damn well what I want to talk to him about. I want that fucking gun, and I want to know why he bought it from my former drug dealer in the first place. More importantly, I need to know exactly what he has planned.

But Will is a master of avoidance, much like Mom. He not only resembles our mother, with his dark-blond hair and vivid green eyes, but he thinks like her, as well. Too bad for him I'm a step ahead of that shit.

"Fine," I say between bites. "Kay and I will watch the movie with you guys."

Kay, who's been quiet up to this point, says, "Yeah, a movie sounds good." She directs her attention to Will. "What movie were you planning on watching?"

I chuckle. My girl is always backing me up. I know she is as sleepy as me, which is *very* sleepy, but she'll do this for me. And she'll do this for Will.

Dear bro, however, doesn't see it quite that way.

"Whatever," he grumbles. "I guess we'll pick something out after Cass gets here."

Cassie arrives a short while later. She and Kay, who hit it off beautifully in Ohio, hug and squeal like they haven't seen each other in years. Will and I, in a rare moment of perfect understanding, look at each other and roll our eyes.

"Girls," Will murmurs so only I can hear. "Talk about

fucking emotional."

"That's for sure," I concur.

After Kay and Cassie are done gushing about how great it is that Kay is in Las Vegas, we retire to the family room. When my eyes fall on all the state-of-the-art electronics, the plush leather furnishings, and the full bar taking up one entire wall, I mumble to myself, "This fucking house is killing me. Unbelievable."

Yeah, I'm still coming to grips with the numerous displays of wealth. I mean, I'm happy and all that the money helps Will to live a more comfortable life. God knows this is way better than the lives we were leading before I left Vegas. Still, I think all this easily available money has spoiled my brother to some extent.

Kay leans in to me and asks for what feels like the hundredth time today, "Are you okay?"

"Just great," I reply. When our eyes meet, however, I know she sees my resentment. I don't want to feel this way, but I can't help it. After our father died, what remained of our family was thrown into abject poverty. We even lived in a fucking minivan for a time.

When we finally made it to an apartment—a hovel, really—Mom was always leaving Will with me. Gambling and men were her top priorities by then. As a result, we never really got back on our feet.

But, now, Mom lives like a queen. And, yeah, it bothers me.

Kay caresses my arm. She tries to soothe me as we settle in next to Cassie and my brother on the mile-long sofa.

Will picks up the remote and scans through the movie options. "Suggestions, anyone?" he queries.

I don't give a fuck what we watch, I think. But I don't say a word; I'm only here to keep an eye on Will and his girlfriend. And, of course, I'm also waiting for an opportunity to talk to the little shit before this day is over.

Cassie, seated between Kay and Will, leans toward Kay and asks, "Have you ever seen 'Bridesmaids'?"

Before Kay can respond, Will chimes in with, "Aw, come on, Cass. Don't start with that chick flick shit. If we're going to watch something like that, let's go with the latest 'Hangover' movie."

"I say we vote on it," Cassie suggests.

Will grumbles an unhappy "okay."

When I abstain from casting an opinion or a vote, "Bridesmaids" win.

Will is clearly not happy with me. From the far end of the sofa, he grumps, "Dude, I thought you had my back."

"I always have your back," I snap, my words laden with double-meaning.

"Yeah, just not when I actually want you to," he volleys back.

"This is bullshit," I mutter.

"For real," Will scoffs. And then he acts like I'm not here, chatting with Cassie and Kay only. I'm here to save the kid from himself, and this is the thanks I get.

"You know what, Will?" I say when he continues to ignore me. "Fuck you."

I'm being a dick, but exhaustion and frustration have left me short-fused. I lean forward, with every intention of getting up and leaving, but Kay stops me when she rests her hand on my jean-clad knee. "Chase, don't," she says, her voice pleading. "Just stay."

It is obvious both Will and Cassie are listening in on our exchange, even though their eyes remain on the just-starting movie.

With reluctance, I settle back on the sofa and sigh. "This is going to be one long night."

And I'm right—it turns out to be one long night indeed. First, the movie feels like it lasts forever. It's funny and all—don't get me wrong—but I just can't get into it.

My mind is on one thing only — Will. I need to talk to him before my mother and Greg return tomorrow. I absolutely want the gun in my possession, safely out of Will's reach. He's far too impulsive.

Cassie seems in good spirits, I take note as the movie plays. That observation leads me to assume she's not been bothered by her perverted stepdad since the last time he harassed her. Still, I wish Kay could get Cassie alone for a few minutes. Cassie trusts Kay and confides in her. I'm sure my girl would have more info in ten minutes than if I spent a whole day talking with my evasive brother.

But there's no time for talking of any kind. After the movie is over, Cassie stands up, grabs her purse, and announces she has to go.

Will immediately jumps up and offers to walk her to her car.

And then they're gone.

"Great," I say on a long sigh.

"Maybe you can talk to Will when he comes back in," Kay offers.

I scrub my hand down my face. "Yeah, maybe."

"What's wrong?"

"I'm just tired, is all."

"Would you rather come up to bed with me?" Kay wants to know. "You can talk with Will in the morning. What time are your mom and Greg due back in town?"

"Sometime in the afternoon," I tell her and then, sighing, I add, "Look, I'm going to wait for Will, babe. Just go on upstairs without me."

Kay reluctantly stands to go, but I can't let her leave just yet.

I stand up next to her, my body towering over her tiny form. I love Kay's smallness. I love that her body appears so fragile, but it's actually Goddamn strong. She accepts whatever I give her, be it physically or emotionally. We've had our ups and downs, and not just under the covers.

But under the covers is all I can think of at the moment. I'm mostly gentle with Kay, with that delicate frame, but I can fuck her hard and she loves it.

Jesus, I'd like to fuck her hard right now, just to take out all the frustration I'm feeling.

"Hey" — she nudges my thigh with her hip — "what are you thinking about?"

Raising an eyebrow in a suggestive manner, I say, "Wouldn't you like to know?"

She says my name, leaning her forehead on my chest. I feel her breathing me in. It's just another way this woman consumes me. I place my hand under her chin, nudging lightly until she's looking up at me. Lowering my lips to hers, I shower her in kisses — wet, raw, passionate kisses with the promise of much, much more.

When both of us are practically panting, we break apart.

"I better go upstairs," she says in a low voice.

Wanton lust darkens her eyes, and I palm her ass with my large hand, giving her a quick squeeze. "I'll be up in a little while," I assure her.

Kay leaves, giving me time to simmer down. Pacing the floor helps. And then, a few minutes later, when Will returns to the family room, I am fine.

I'm kind of surprised he has returned, and I let out a cough.

"What?" he says. "Did you think you were going to have to hunt me down?"

"I kind of did think exactly that." I admit.

He snorts, "This house ain't that big, bro."

He's right about that; I'd find him no matter what.

Will and I start to sit down on the sofa at the same time, which makes him laugh. "Go ahead," he says, smiling.

I sit and he follows. Will is still smiling, but that shit

turns to a frown when I say, "Will, a gun? Really? What the fuck were you thinking?"

I expect an argument, an epic one, so I gear up accordingly. But surprisingly I get no grief. Instead, Will says resignedly, "I'll give you the damn thing if it'll make you quit nagging me about it."

Before I can even reply — which would be a *hell, yes* — he jumps up and leaves the room, tossing over his shoulder before he's out of sight, "Don't worry. I'm coming right back."

I'm rather stunned Will is giving up so easily. This is so not like my brother.

He returns in mere minutes, a revolver in his hand. "It's not loaded," he says as he hands the gun to me, butt-first.

I look over the pistol. Hmm, it appears to be an Old West collector's revolver.

"You got this from Kyle Tanner?" I ask, suspicious.

"Yep, that's what he sold me."

Will glances away, and I wonder: *Is this really the right gun?* I can't imagine drug-addled Tanner dealing in nineteenth-century weaponry. But then again, he may have stolen it from somewhere before he sold it to Will.

Whatever the case, something feels off.

Nonetheless, I say to Will, "Okay. Well, thanks for turning it over to me."

"I wasn't going to do anything crazy with it, anyway," Will declares. "I bought it to keep with me for when I was with Cassie. Figured if Paul showed up, and I brandished that" — he nods to the gun — "it might scare him away for good."

"Will," I breathe out. "You can't threaten people with guns."

"I hardly think of him as a person," Will scoffs.

"Look, Will," I say, sighing. "Yes, Paul is an asshole,

but you can't threaten him with a deadly weapon. You'll end up getting yourself into more trouble than he is in."

"The police are still looking for him," Will says, "so I hardly doubt that."

Paul violated the restraining order against him when he stopped Cassie on the side of the road last week and almost molested her. Thank God for the passing car that made him stop. The police have been searching for Paul ever since, but to no avail. Paul's ability to sneak around doing this shit is what makes Will crazy.

"Still," I tell my brother, "just let the police handle things."

"I'm going to, Chase." Will says. "I promise."

Yeah, I think, *we'll see about that.*

After Will goes up to bed, I sit in the family room alone for a while. It's just me and my thoughts, which leaves me feeling restless.

I could—and should—head upstairs and go to bed. Warm Kay is waiting up there for me. I can lose myself in her like I did before dinner.

And I will, but not yet.

I wander around the house for a bit, checking out things on the first floor. Every room is spacious and meticulously decorated. I stroll through the living room, which doesn't look like it's used all that often. Then I'm on to the downstairs bedrooms, including Mom and Greg's room. Next, I walk through Greg's study and then amble through a small library. When I'm back in the dining room, I turn this way and that, until I ultimately decide to wind my way to the kitchen. There I come upon a laundry room/mudroom combo in the far corner. The door to the garage is in there. Curious as to what kind of cars Mom and Greg are driving these days, I step into the mudroom and swing open the door leading to the massive garage area.

"Wow," I mouth as my gaze sweeps over four spots, all occupied with very nice vehicles. There's a Mercedes, a Porsche, a Range Rover, and a sweet Dodge Challenger, cherry red with white stripes. I assume that car is for Will for when he turns sixteen next year. He hasn't mentioned the car, though, and you think he would. Still, if I know my mother—and I sure as hell do—this is just like her. If there's one thing Abby excels at, it is keeping secrets. She probably bamboozled Will into thinking the Challenger is Greg's car. But I know how she plots and plans and surprising Will with a car on his sixteenth birthday is just her style. It's so typical of Mom to think a pricy gift might make up for all her years of neglect.

"Think again," I snort as I step into the multi-vehicle garage.

I notice there's a fifth parking spot, but it appears empty. Until I walk over to it.

Just as I'm passing the red Challenger I catch sight of something I never thought I'd ever see again, something I assumed was long gone.

I stare long and hard at my father's old 1960 Indian Matchless motorcycle, muttering, "Shit, no way."

Mom told me everything was gone. Hell, we sold off ninety-nine percent of our belongings when we went bankrupt. I remember those dark days all too well. So where has Dad's old motorcycle been all this time? And what's my mother doing with it parked in Greg's garage?

Much like baby brother, it seems Mom is keeping secrets, too.

FOUR

Kay

I WAIT and I wait in the upstairs bedroom, but Chase doesn't come to bed. Eventually, I nod off, but only for a short while. I can't sleep in this unknown house, this too-quiet home. I'm used to the farmhouse back in Harmony Creek, and my apartment above Chase's garage. There, in both places, when the windows are open you can hear the sounds of the outdoors, teeming with life. Crickets chirping, frogs singing down at the creek, and the occasional call of a nighthawk. But here in this closed-up, gated community, all I hear is the low hum of whole-house air conditioning.

Not exactly soothing for a country girl at heart.

When I can't take another minute of artificially generated sound, I get out of bed. I took off all my clothes before lying down, in anticipation of some quality time with Chase, so I now take a minute to dig out a short, silky robe from my still-packed suitcase.

Once I find the robe and am covered, I knot the pale-pink sash around my waist.

Then, I start down the stairs.

The first level of the house is illuminated with here and there nightlights. The only room with a big light on appears to be the kitchen. Chase is not in there, but I hear noise coming from what I assume is a garage area.

Concluding that Chase must be in there, I step over a big pile of Will's unwashed clothes, in the center of the laundry room, and swing open a door leading into what I discover is a huge, multi-car garage.

"Wow," I mutter as I take in all the expensive cars.

On the far end of the massive garage space, I hear Chase call out, "Hey, babe, come on in. I'm over here."

He sounds so cheerful, unlike earlier in the night. I'm glad his mood has improved; I guess things went well with Will. But what has brought Chase out to the garage? Something he sounds pleased with, that much I can tell.

I walk past all the fancy cars and stroll over to where Chase is crouched down, his hand moving appreciatively over the curve of an old motorcycle. The bike appears to be a classic of some sort—completely restored, however.

"Wow," I say as I reach Chase, nodding to the bike. "That is really nice."

"Yeah, it is," he says wistfully, his hand still but remaining on the bike.

"Does it belong to Greg?"

"No, it was my dad's."

Whoa, no way.

"I thought all your father's things were gone?" I carefully inquire.

"Yeah," Chase says on a long exhale. "I thought so, too." And then, a little lower and more to himself than to me, he murmurs, "Shit, Dad loved this thing."

I move closer to Chase. "Did he ever take you for a ride

on it?" I ask.

"All the time, Kay."

Chase looks up and smiles at me, and I cross my arms over my chest and smile back.

"Do you, by chance, know how to drive it?" I inquire.

"Actually, I do." He laughs lightly. "Dad used to always tell me not to let Mom know he was taking me out to the desert all the time and letting me drive this thing."

"That must have been fun," I say, laughing.

"The best," Chase agrees as his gaze returns to the bike.

He appears so happy. Discovering that this little part of his dad is still around has revived Chase; he looks less worried, less stressed. Chase has always been intense, but when I first met him he didn't have the worries of Will weighing him down. Though he was burdened with his own struggles, Chase was more carefree. His demeanor now reminds me of those early days of getting to know him—lunches at the diner, him stealing my hair tie and me running after him, and me taking off with his last lemon-lime soda while he chased me down.

And then there was that first kiss.

I shiver with excitement at the memory. Oh, how I loved, and still love, to let Chase catch me. Whether for first kisses, or for catching me when I fall, he is always there. Suddenly, I realize Chase needs what I once sought—he needs to forgive himself. I don't think he even realizes it, but there's something in him that truly believes he could have somehow prevented his father's suicide all those years ago. Chase blames himself for the faults of his father, as well as the subsequent sins of his mother. He feels guilt for going to prison, guilt for what he sees as his abandoning Will.

Chase helped me through my fires of Hell—I would never have forgiven myself for my role in my little sister's death had it not been for his love and forgiveness. The least I can do now is stand by him while he faces these demons of his own. I thought up to now that love alone would be enough, but we can't take advantage of this gift we've been given. Piling our past on top of our love will only weigh it down.

Chase needs resolution.

Like me, he will forever be sullied, but we can live with that. The smudges on our souls can't be washed away, but we have learned to accept that. However, the weight of regret over things we had no control over still looms and is a threat to our love.

I don't regret my past any longer; I accept it as part of me. Chase, though, remains tortured by his past. Facing unresolved issues with his father is a start for Chase; I see this now. Finding this old motorcycle is good, very good.

Sometimes healing comes from the most unlikely of sources.

I crouch down next to Chase and leaning my head on his shoulder, I say, "Hey, maybe we can take the bike out while we're here. Do you think it runs?"

Chase turns away from the bike. He stands, pulling me up with him as we face one another. With my hands in his, he says, "It looks like it's still in working order, and I think taking it out is a great idea, Kay."

"Good," I reply. "I think so, too."

Sadness, though, clouds Chase's eyes as he tightens his hands on mine. "I'm trying to work through these problems, babe," he says. "And I know it's been hard on us lately."

"We'll get through it," I reply.

Holding my gaze, his troubled blues question, *And if we don't, then what?*

"We will," I whisper, responding to his unspoken fear. "We always do."

He lets go of me and scrubs a hand down his face. "I

hope you're right," he mutters.

I want to change the subject—for now—so I ask, "Did you talk with Will after I went upstairs?"

"I did," he says slowly.

He then gives me the rundown of their conversation.

"Hmm," I murmur, frowning. "Do you really think the gun he gave you is the gun Kyle sold to him?"

Chase shrugs his wide shoulders. "I don't know. I sure as hell hope it is."

In a low voice, I quietly say, "If not, though, then it means Will still has a gun in his possession."

Chase sighs. "Yeah, I know. That's why I've been thinking we should stay in town for a while."

"We do have three more weeks off from work. School starts after Labor Day," I offer helpfully.

I work as a first-grade teacher at Holy Trinity Elementary, the church-run school. And Chase works for the church as a sort of handyman. We don't have to return to work until September since my summer secretarial job ended, and Father Maridale gave Chase time off to work out this thing with Will.

Chase pulls me to him, his hands reaching down and slipping under the pale-pink silk of my robe. "You're okay with staying, then?"

His fingers graze over my thigh, trailing up higher and higher. "Uh-huh," I gasp when he reaches and squeezes my ass cheeks lightly.

"Baby," he says.

His tone is smug, knowing what his touch does to me.

"Don't stop," I whisper.

He doesn't stop. Chase nuzzles my neck, his lips soft and wet. "This little robe is cute," he murmurs against my skin, his breath the lightest of tickles. He finds the tie at my waist and adds, "But I think it has to go."

"Yes," I agree. "Good idea."

Making short work of the loose knot, Chase slides the silky material down my body till it's just a puddle of pink fabric on the garage floor.

"You're so beautiful, baby girl," he tells me as his eyes scan every inch of my bared-for-him body.

When Chase dips a finger between my legs, I moan.

He chuckles and says in return, "Always so ready for me, aren't you?"

It's true; I am always ready for him.

"I am," I say. "I want you, always."

Chase glances around the room, like he's trying to decide where he wants to take me.

Anywhere, I long to tell him. *You can take me anywhere, because you already have me everywhere.*

He eyes the bike for a few seconds, but decides against it. Slowly, he walks me backward to the parked Porsche.

"It does have a nice, swoopy hood," I say, which makes him laugh.

We reach the car and as he leans me back against it, he rasps, "It sure does."

I prop myself up on the hood on my elbows and ask, "Is this your mom's car, or Greg's?"

"I don't know," Chase says as he unzips his jeans, "and I don't really care."

He slides his jeans and boxer briefs low on his hips, freeing his magnificent hardness. I reach out and wrap my hand around the silky smooth skin while I squeeze at the solid length beneath. "I want you right now," I tell him.

Like Chase, I don't care whose car this is. All I want is for Chase to spread me wide on the hood and fill me as only he can do.

He pulls his T-shirt over his head. That move is for me; he knows I like to touch the wings tattooed on his back when we're together like this.

I lean all the way back and scoot up on metal so smooth my skin doesn't stick or stop. I just glide.

Chase leans over me. His hand rests next to my head, the muscles in his left arm straining and bunching as he supports his weight. With his free hand, he does what I love to watch him do—handles his cock.

I watch as he strokes once, twice, and then positions himself at my core. I place my hand on the tattoo scrolling around his left bicep. I've read the words a million times, but I read them again, out loud. "As I stand before you, judge me not."

"Fitting words," he says.

"For both of us," I say, and then I add, "I love your tattoos so much."

"I know you do, baby," Chase replies.

With his engorged tip at my entrance, Chase guides himself into me inch-by-inch. I writhe and arch at the slow but delicious torture of him filling my small body. When he's in me as far as he can go, he makes me look up at him.

His gaze is questioning, tortured. I want Chase to find peace. And I certainly want to help him, no matter what that might entail.

Chase starts to move, his gaze never leaving mine. "I need you," he whispers at last.

"I'm here," I whisper back, gasping when he thrusts into me more roughly. "I'm here, Chase. I'm here."

I know he hears me, but from the frantic way he keeps plunging into me, I don't think he really *hears* me. He drives into me like he's branding me, marking me. He's doing everything he can to make me his forever.

Doesn't he know I will always be his?

Logically, I believe he knows. But there's something deep in Chase that makes him fear I will leave him, just as he's been left in the past.

Never, ever will that happen, I long to say.

But he needs more than words. He needs to learn it on his own by overcoming his fears. I just don't know if Chase sees as clearly as I do the things which haunt him.

FIVE

Chase

F I keep this up, I am going to lose Kay.

Am I being irrational?

I don't know. But even if she doesn't leave me, she deserves more than this. I need to confront and work through my issues, just as I encouraged her to do. Maybe if I quell these demons haunting me, I'll finally be the better man I've been striving to become.

After all, Kay deserves nothing less than my best.

I spend the morning in the garage, getting the old Indian bike ready to go. It's in good working order, but it's not fully road-ready. I work fast, as my goal is to have this thing out of here before my mother and her husband get home.

Truth is, I have no burning desire to be part of the welcoming committee. Let Will have the honor of bringing Mom and Greg up to speed. Little bro can figure out how best to inform them that Kay and I are staying in Las

Vegas…and that we plan to stay here for a while.

Though I'm sure Will won't be divulging exactly *why* Kay and I came to town.

Yeah, I'd place a Vegas bet on that shit.

Whatever, I think, sighing. Bottom line is that while all that is going down, I'll be with Kay. We're taking the bike out together. Shortly after we woke early this morning, I tossed out the idea…and Kay liked it.

"Where should we go?" she called out over her shoulder as she made her way to the bathroom adjoined to our bedroom.

After I retrieved my boxers, I walked to the doorway. Kay was standing in front of the basin, brushing her teeth. She looked cute as all get-out, hair all mussed and still sleepy-eyed.

It took me a minute to respond, but finally as I leaned on the doorframe, I said, "Anywhere you want to go, baby girl. Your wish is my command."

"You have to pick," she said, turning to face me after she rinsed out her mouth. "You know Las Vegas better than I do."

Yes, I sure do, I thought.

I'm still thinking the same thing too—here in the garage, two hours later. However, the Las Vegas I know oh-so-well sure isn't something I'd ever show Kay. Sure, she knows my past—most of it, anyway—but there's no need to revisit the pit stops I traveled along the way. Sadly, my Las Vegas tour would be filled with dark alleys, darker apartments, and the darkest of nights. All shaded in tones of addiction, sorrow, and despair.

Would I ever want to show beautiful, gentle Kay where I used to score coke, coke that made my head feel like it was exploding?

No way.

Or maybe I could spin her by the old apartment and

point out where Will and I spent many a night alone while Mom was off gambling? Hell, I could take her to the convenience store around the corner and point out the aisle where I once stole a can of Spam. Don't laugh. That can of mystery meat provided a makeshift holiday dinner that year when Mom forgot to come home on Christmas Eve.

Would I subject Kay to that memory of mine? Short answer: *No.*

In fact, I wish I could block out some of those memories myself. I don't like recalling how Will and I ate the Spam I stole out of the can that year.

But I do remember, I remember it all, including how Will cried the whole time, saying he wanted his mother.

Slumping down next to the bike, the distant memory leaves me feeling choked up.

Fuck. That Christmas had to be one of the worst.

Following our crappy Spam dinner, Will and I went to sleep. We were trying to forget it was a even a holiday, but Christmas Day, of course, arrived.

We couldn't stop it, we couldn't stop anything back then. We were caught up in a downward spiral.

When Will woke up, he asked me where all our presents were.

I could not bring myself to tell him there were none. So, instead, I ran around the apartment, gathering up the shit we already owned — Will's toothpaste, my shaving cream, Will's tree-house sketch, my sketch pad, some other random shit. I wrapped everything up in colorful comic pages I ripped from an old newspaper.

Will knew none of the stuff was new, but he played along. In fact, that kid and I opened those gifts like they were brand-spanking-new treasures.

And it wasn't so bad, not really. It was okay until Will starting crying, saying he wanted his mother.

But Mom wasn't there, like so many other days.

She came home a day later. Until then, though, it was only me. And unfortunately I was never enough.

How could I—a boy myself at the time—fill a void left by two parents, one dead, and one who may as well have been.

Jesus, this life I've lived.

Kay thinks I can figure it all out, find myself some peace. She believes somewhere inside of me I will know where I need to start in order to get back to this side of right. But when you're facing not just past demons, but present ones as well, let's just say things get tricky.

Thank God at least Will seems better. Having Cassie over last night, our little talk, it's all keeping my brother steady. I mean, I think it is. In any case, so far there have been no drugs, no meltdowns, and no seeking vigilante justice.

Still, I'm shaky on the gun. I only hope the firearm Will gave to me is the same one Kyle sold him. I have no choice, though, but to accept that it was.

Kay arrives a few minutes later, just as I'm tinkering with a few final adjustments on the motorcycle. She looks radiant and ready for the day in dark jeans, a sexy red V-neck tee, and black low-heel ankle boots.

I stand and hand her a helmet. "You sure look ready to hit the road," I say.

Her hair is in a ponytail and she tucks it up on her head as she slides on the helmet.

"Yep, I sure am," she replies. "I'm ready for you to take me wherever you want to go."

"Oh, that leaves a lot of possibilities," I joke, winking at her.

I feel better now that Kay is with me.

She rolls her eyes, but she's smiling at me the whole time. "Let's go, tiger," she says.

I'm still not sure where to go, so we hit the road with no set path. As we head north of Vegas, I let the road be my guide. The hum of the bike, the rippling sound of the wind, cruising through the open desert is hypnotic.

When I finally take note of where we've ended up, I discover we are in the same area my dad used to let me drive the bike, the same bike we're on this sunny, fine day.

It's quiet and desolate out here in the middle of nowhere, but in the best kind of way. It's blue skies and open road, until I catch sight of an old general store—the only sign of civilization for miles.

I yell back to Kay, "Hey, are you thirsty? There's a shop up ahead."

The scorching sun has been beating down on our backs for over an hour, so I'm not one bit surprised when Kay replies, "Yeah, definitely. Let's stop for a while, Chase."

It's decided, and we pull in and park at the general store, before going in for our drinks. After paying, and armed with two big bottles of soda—orange for my girl and lemon-lime for me—we push open the flimsy screen door at the entrance and collapse onto two wooden rocking chairs out on the front porch of the establishment.

The porch is a few steps up from the parking lot, affording us a very nice view of the desert horizon—jagged peaks and valleys, brown and dusty, covered in all varieties of cacti.

"It's nice out here," Kay says.

"It is," I agree.

We kick back, and as we sip at our ice-cold drinks, a little brown lizard on the railing runs by.

"Aw, cute," Kay says, smiling over at me. "Is that the kind you and Will used to catch?"

Chuckling, I lean back in my chair and reply, "Yeah, but let's get that story straight. *I* was the one who used to catch the lizards. Will was adept at one thing only—

scaring them away."

Kay laughs just as the wind whips up, sending dirt and sand in the parking lot spiraling up into little, mini tornadoes.

Over the noise, she says, "How can I forget, Chase. That lizard-tale was one of the first stories you ever told me."

I close my eyes. "It was, wasn't it?"

"Yep," she says quietly, "it was one of the first...and one of the best."

We remain quiet, lost in our thoughts.

Kay has always loved that story — the tale of Will and the evasive lizards. I shared that memory — one of the best — during one of our first lunch dates. That day now seems so far away, even though, in reality, it was just a few short months ago.

I sigh. This woman and I have been through so much together that the weeks feel like years.

I send a glance Kay's way, and find her shielding her eyes from the sun while biting her lower lip.

Is she thinking about our first days spent together, getting to know one another?

With a contemplative expression on her beautiful face, one that leads me to think she may very well be thinking the same thing, she slips her sunglasses from where they are perched on her head to down over her eyes.

With her eyewear in place, she glances over at me. It's hard, though, to discern what's going on behind those dark lenses, so I ask, "What are you thinking about?"

After taking a long sip of pop, she says, "I was thinking it feels like we've come such a long way in such a short time."

I can't disagree, since I was just thinking pretty much the same thing.

"It does," I agree. "It sure does."

I take a long pull from my soda, feeling a bit contemplative myself.

This little store is not only close to where I learned to ride the bike. Out here, in this part of the desert, we're not far from where my dad is buried.

Maybe I drove in this direction for a purpose. Maybe I did it self-consciously. Maybe Kay's right and I *do* know where I need to go to start healing.

Tentatively—I still don't know if this is such a good idea—I ask her if she'd be okay with stopping by the cemetery.

"Just for a minute or two," I say in a rushed tone.

"Of course, Chase. I don't mind stopping at all." She sends a supportive smile my way. "And we can stay as long as you like."

"Thanks, babe," I murmur.

After a beat, Kay adds. "You know, I've actually wanted to see where your Dad is buried for a long time now."

"Hmm…" I trail off.

I'm sure what Kay is saying is true, I'm sure of this for a few reasons. First, she is well-aware the stone angel at my Dad's grave was the inspiration for the kneeling angel inked on my back. She's curious to see the real thing, no doubt. And then there's the fact she has shared with me *everything* about the little sister she lost a few years back. She not only took me to where Sarah is buried many times, but she's also shared with me the memories she holds closest to her heart.

Sharing things with me, taking me to a place she holds sacred, those things helped Kay heal. Maybe sharing with her my dad's final resting place will be a starting point for me.

"Let's get going," I say to Kay as we finish our sodas.

We're back on the bike in minutes and heading to the

cemetery. We are quiet on the way, and we remain silent as we walk to the grave.

"Here it is," I say, breaking the silence, my voice cracking since we've reached my father's final resting spot.

I am slightly nervous, having not been out here in so long, but I'm also somewhat soothed.

It's been a long time, Dad. Shit, the things I've done.

"You used to come here every day?" Kay asks, breaking me out of my wandering thoughts.

"Yeah," I reply, nodding as I shift my weight from one foot to the other. "I'd take the bus. The stop for the one that came out here wasn't far from our apartment. I still had to walk a bit once I was dropped off. But I made the trip almost every day, for, like, forever."

"Did it help?"

Kay looks over at me. Her sunglasses are up on her head again, but unlike earlier at the store, she doesn't lower them to shield the sun.

She wants to see me; she wants to see my reactions. And she wants me to see her, so I know for sure she's here for me.

"I don't know if coming out here helped," I hedge. "Maybe...but I really don't know for sure."

"You don't know?" Kay chuckles. "Come on, Chase, be honest with me."

I take a breath, and then I tell her the truth. "Okay. I don't think it helped all that much. I was so lost back then, babe."

I glance up at the stone angel; she's as imposing as ever.

"What were you searching for?" Kay asks, her eyes on the angel as well.

"I was searching for answers."

Kay reaches for me.

As I take Kay's hand, I realize something. Under the watchful eyes of the looming stone angel, I no longer feel lost, not like I did back then. I'm not alone anymore. I have Kay with me, by my side, always, as things are meant to be.

I squeeze my love's hand and smile.

Quietly, she asks, "What were you *really* seeking back then, Chase?"

With my free hand, I rake my fingers through my hair. "It's not important," I mutter.

But Kay's not having any of my evasive shit. She frees her hand from mine and turns to me, making me face her.

"Chase," she says. "I know that's not true. Just tell me."

"No judgments?"

"Never."

"Just checking," I say.

"Quit stalling." Kay smacks my arm.

"Okay, okay." Hand through my hair again. "I wanted to know why my dad left us. I used to question how he could end it all like that. I mean, shit, he had a wife who adored him and two sons who thought the sun rose and set on him." I shake my head. "How does a man throw something that good away? Some people go through their whole lives looking for love like that, and I just don't get it." My voice cracks and Kay wraps her little arms around me.

"Chase," she murmurs, her cheek pressed to my chest. "I wish I knew why people do the crazy things they do. If I could give you some answers, believe me, I would."

"I believe you," I whisper.

Looking up at me slowly, her caramels liquid and bleary with unshed tears, she continues. "People do desperate things when their lives are falling apart. Your dad's world was in turmoil. I'm sure, though, through it all he still loved you."

She's told me that before, but I'm still in doubt.

"Yeah," I bite out, "he sure had a shitty way of showing

it."

I have to pull away from Kay's embrace; it's too comforting. I can't do comfort, not right now, so I walk away. I am determined to hang onto this anger. After all, it's what I know best.

Kay, undeterred, is on my ass.

"He had his own demons, Chase," she says breathlessly from behind me. Her steps become faster and faster as she attempts to keep up with me. "His failures led him to take his own life. What happened with your father had absolutely nothing to do with you...or with Will. You and your brother were just children, for God's sake."

Bitter tears I've left unshed begin to fall.

My steps slow.

Slow, slower...

And then I can't go on.

I sit my ass down next to some random stranger's grave and place my head in my hands.

"He was a fucking prick to leave us like that," I yell out. "He didn't care that I still needed him, he didn't care..."

Kay kneels down in front of me. "Chase, Chase, I'm so sorry." Her hand is on my forearm. "You're always trying to be so strong for everyone. You needed your dad back then, and you still need someone. Your dad isn't here, but I am. Let me help you. Please, let me be here for you."

Her hands go to my shoulders, urging me to raise my head and meet her soft gaze.

But I can't.

"Please, Chase," she continues, her hands shaking my shoulders lightly. "You've done so much for me. Let me be here for you." She chokes back a sob. "Just let me love you. Please, baby, please."

I finally find the strength to meet her gaze. "I do let you love me," I tell her.

"So, let me love you *more*."

That gets me smiling. And it makes me want to tease her some to lighten the mood. "What would all this extra loving involve, exactly?"

When I raise a brow suggestively, she swats my arm.

"Stop," she says. But she's smiling the whole time. "I'm trying to be serious here."

"I know, and you *have* helped me. You've helped me more than you'll ever know, Kay. Just having you here with me, it makes me see things differently. I realized something when we first arrived here at the cemetery, when we were walking quietly to Dad's grave."

"What did you realize?"

I take a breath. "That I don't view this place the way I used to."

"What do you mean?"

Her voice is soft, pleading, so I try to explain. "When I look around"—I make a sweeping motion with my hand—"at all of this, I see something new. I used to come here and I would see nothing but grave after grave, a desert wasteland. To me, this place was death on top of more death."

"Chase..."

"But here's the thing," I continue. "Look around, baby." I point to vibrant desert sage, a big barrel cactus, and a bush with bright yellow blooms. "There is life here, too. There's life all around us."

"Even in the desert," Kay marvels as she glances left and right.

"Even in the desert," I repeat. "And do you know why?"

She looks at me, her gaze questioning.

"Because these plants, these things that are alive, they adapted. They grew and changed. These living things evolved to how they needed to be in this harsh environment." Sighing, I add, "Maybe that's what I need to learn how to do."

Kay replies, "I think you *have* been doing that, Chase. Since the day you got out of prison, you've been changing and adapting."

She's right, but I tell her the truth of it. "It sure as hell hasn't been easy."

"Nothing worthwhile ever is."

She would know.

I rise to my knees and cup her face in my hands. "How'd you end up being so smart, Kay Stanton?"

Shy girl says nothing, but the compliment makes her blush like crazy. And I love it.

"So cute," I murmur as I rub my thumbs over her pink cheeks.

"Oh, stop," she says.

Her blush goes from pink to red, and she tries to wiggle away. But I'm not letting her get away. My hands remain, cupping her face. She always feels so breakable beneath my strength. I can't help but be amazed.

"How can you be so strong, yet feel so fragile?" I ask.

"I'm not so very fragile," she says with a sly smile.

"No," — I smile back at her — "I guess you're not."

And she's not. But she's strong in more than just the sexual ways she's intimating. Kay has strength and fortitude for the both of us. That's why I know that beyond today's first step — and it's been a good first step, as I finally feel some peace — I will keep making progress.

After all, if I can find signs of life in the Nevada desert, then I can surely find signs of life among my own ruins.

SIX

Kay

WHEN Chase and I return to the house, his mom and Greg are home. We step into the entry hall tentatively, where all of us kind of stand around, sizing each other up.

Greg speaks first, uttering a quick, "Hello, nice to meet you." He shakes both my and Chase's hand formally, and then declares he is retiring to his study.

"I have paperwork to get caught up on," he says to Abby.

He's so much older and more reserved-looking than I expected him to be.

Abby replies "Okay, dear," and then Greg is gone.

With her husband out of the room, Chase's mother turns her full attention to her eldest. "Chase," she exhales dramatically. "Oh, baby, come here."

Chase doesn't move an inch, so Abby sighs and goes to him. She encircles him in an awkward hug, clinging to him like she hasn't seen him in years. But I know Chase's mother saw him in April, the day he was released from prison.

"Oh, sweetie, sweetie," Abby coos, her dark-blonde hair tumbling from her loose bun.

Abby Gartner—or rather, Abby Vintner nowadays— is an attractive woman. She's thin and petite. Her sons apparently inherited their height from their dad. But it's not all Jack Gartner genetics that have been passed down to his sons. Will definitely has Abby's green eyes.

"Mom, come on." Chase pulls away from his mom. "Please. I think that's enough."

Abby is far from done, though. In fact, there's so much fanfare in the next five minutes from his mother that Chase ends up walking away.

"I can't do this right now," he says as he heads for the stairs. "I'm going up to take a shower."

"You'll be down for dinner, though, right, baby?" Abby sounds like a wounded puppy.

"Yep," Chase replies, his tone clipped.

And then he's up the stairs and out of sight, leaving me standing in the entry hall with his overwrought mom.

Wow. Chase may have made peace with his dad today, but I can see there's much work ahead when it comes to reaching a common ground with his mother.

Abby eyes me appraisingly for a full two minutes. "Hmm," she says at last. "So, you're Kay."

"Yes, ma'am."

"Well." She blows out a breath, and then surprises me when she says, "I have to say I think you may be the best thing that has happened to my son. He's a little high-strung at the moment"—*he's* high-strung? I almost blurt out—"but overall, he seems...different around you."

"Oh?" I raise a brow, curious as to her perceptions. "How does he seem different?"

Abby taps a pink manicured nail to her chin in a thoughtful manner. "Chase is definitely calmer than he was a few months ago," she begins. "And, despite his irritation with me a few minutes ago, he seems more grounded."

Okay, so this woman is not completely flighty and unaware. She's perceptive when it suits her, or so it seems.

I relax a bit.

She relaxes too, and after a few more minutes of idle chit-chat, Abby asks me to accompany her to the kitchen.

"Come on," she says, turning and beckoning. "You can help me get dinner started."

I'd much rather head upstairs to make sure Chase is all right, but what can I do? Should I tell Abby no? I don't think that would be prudent since I'm staying in her house, so I keep my mouth shut and follow her to the kitchen.

When we start prepping for dinner, I discover something new about Chase's mother—she's quite bossy.

She hands me three large, ripe tomatoes and says, "Here, chop these up. Finely chopped is what I prefer. I don't like my tomatoes too chunky."

"Okay, then," I say. "Finely chopped it is."

I barely get my response out before Abby is talking right over me. "Now put them in the salad when you're done." She pushes a big wooden bowl she's just filled with a bagged salad down the counter to me.

Eight minutes later, Abby is at the stove, frying chicken. "'Kay," she says, "can you come over here and turn these chicken breasts for me? I need to run out to the back patio for a little air. It feels stuffy in here."

I think it feels fine in the house, but I nonetheless set the salad aside, and say, "Yeah, sure," as I step over to the stove.

When the chicken is just about done, Abby returns. She takes over at the stove, and I get a whiff of cigarette smoke from the deep-rose sheath dress she's wearing.

Hmm…

Chase suspected his mother had not given up smoking. Guess he was correct.

Abby leans away from the stove, frying oil spattering in her wake. She turns down the heat while opening a utility drawer with her other hand. From the drawer, she removes a small bottle of perfume and sprays a little on the tan skin of her wrist, and then on the dress.

"What?" she says as she catches me watching her. "I smoke when I'm stressed, okay?" She brandishes the perfume bottle. "This hides the odor from Greg."

I quickly turn away. Raising a hand, I say, "It's not my business."

"Perhaps not," she replies slowly. "But there's one little problem… Chase also thinks I quit."

"Hmm," I murmur.

In a low, conspiratorial voice, Abby says, "I'd like to keep it that way, Chase thinking I quit. I mean, if that's okay with you, of course."

Oh, no, I am not going down that slippery slope of keeping secrets from Chase for his mother.

She must see hesitation in my expression, as she quickly amends, "You know what, just forget it. I'll tell him the truth myself and just get it over with."

"That would probably be best," I mutter.

Ten minutes later we are all seated at the dining room table. Chase is freshly showered, hair unkempt and damp. Damn, he looks good every second of every day. How does he do that?

I smile, thinking, *that man, he sure is a stunner.*

Chase is wearing a dark-gray T-shirt — one with an old band name on it — and faded jeans. He works the jeans-and-tees look oh-so-well, like he's ready to star in some hot male model spread. And here I sit in the same desert-dusty jeans and V-neck tee from earlier. Suffice it to say, I don't look nearly as good as Chase.

Oh, well, he loves me anyway.

As if to accentuate that point like he's reading my mind, Chase smiles over at me and mouths, "You look beautiful."

I just roll my eyes and laugh.

When everyone is settled, dinner commences.

I watch as Greg picks up the salad tongs and fills his salad bowl with lettuce. Abby, I note, messes with the napkin on her lap. She seems uneasy, waiting for the other shoe to drop. And then I see why when I look over at Chase. He's scanning the chairs around the table, frowning.

"Where's Will?" he sharply asks his mother.

"He won't be joining us for dinner today," she replies, her voice unnaturally light and carefree.

Abby abandons messing with her napkin and instead starts pushing around pieces of chicken on her plate.

"Why isn't Will joining us for dinner?" Chase's voice is anything but light.

Greg clears his throat, but Chase pays him no heed. "Mom," he presses, "where is Will?"

Abby picks up her water glass and takes a long sip. She sets it down carefully and, not meeting Chase's stare, she says, "Your brother went over to Cassie's house for the night. You'll see him tomorrow."

"You gotta be kidding me." Chase sounds incredulous. "He's staying over there the entire night?"

Abby nods.

Chase shakes his head. "You do realize Mrs. Sutter leaves them alone all the time. What do you think they do when there is no supervision?"

Abby shrugs. "I'm sure they talk, watch TV, maybe play a few video games. That's what kids do these days, right?"

Exasperated, Chase blurts out, "You cannot be this fucking clueless, Mom."

"Hey, hey," Greg interjects. "Watch the language at the table, please."

Chase laughs. "Oh, that's rich. I can't say 'fuck,' but it's perfectly okay that fucking is exactly what Will and his girlfriend are probably doing right now."

"Chase!" Abby gasps.

Greg yells, "That's enough!"

Chase ignores them both as he stands and slams his chair into the table. "You're both so fucking blind it's not even funny. No wonder there are problems in this house."

I remain silent, having no right to intervene. I stare down at chicken I no longer have an appetite for and think: *Welcome to a Gartner family dinner.*

SEVEN

Chase

FUCKING Mom, fucking Greg, fucking Will.

Well, maybe not Will. He's been okay.

Or so it seems. Who knows?

All I know is Will was abiding by the rules I set for him and Cassie in Ohio. The only sex going on under my roof was between me and Kay. Clearly, the situation is different here.

But how can my mother be so blind to reality? How she can breeze on in to a place and blow things all to hell within a day? I'll never know. But I do know her actions play a big part in Will's problems.

And I've had it.

I storm in to the fucking five-car garage. Stomping over to the Indian, I take a seat on the cement floor next to the bike. When I notice some dirt on the left shock absorber, near the back tire, I lean toward a nearby shelf on the wall and grab a rag.

Just as I'm wiping and polishing, I hear the opening of a door.

It's either Mom or Kay coming into the garage.

Please be Kay, please be Kay.

"Chase."

Fuck, it's Mom.

"What do you want?" I ask. I don't bother to look up at her, even when she reaches where I'm seated.

"Can we talk?" she quietly asks.

"I don't know," I scoff. "And by the way, where's Kay?"

"She went upstairs. She wanted to come to you, but I asked her to give us a few minutes to talk things out."

"A few minutes to talk things out?" I scoff. "Really? You think we can get this shit straightened out in a few short minutes?"

"Well, no," Mom replies, sighing. "Maybe it'll take more than a few minutes. But how long, Chase? How long will it take before you and I reach some kind of common ground here?"

"Try forever," I snap.

I still haven't looked up at my mother, but I eye her up good when I stand. I have every intention of giving her one final stare-down before taking off. But when I see all the pain in her eyes—true sorrow—I ease up.

I can't do cold-hearted—not right now—so I say in a kinder-than-I'm-feeling tone, "Okay, where do you want to start?"

"Where do you think I want to start, Chase? I want to know what's going on. I want to know why you're really here. Your brother said you and Kay just up and decided to visit. Like, out of the blue." She waves her hand around. "That's pretty random, Chase, even for you. And don't think I'm buying it even for a minute."

I shrug. "I don't know what you're talking about."

My mom lets out a frustrated, "Jesus." And then, after a beat, says, "Don't give me that shit, Chase Michael Gartner. Your brother's been acting shady, and I think you know why. What are you keeping from me? I know something is up with that kid."

Ha, if only she knew. But I'm not sure I'm ready to deal with Mom's histrionics when she learns "that kid" bought a gun in Ohio.

Swiftly, I steer the subject to what caused all the fuss at dinner, thinking the whole while *best to pick your battles carefully.*

"Will and Cassie are having sex, Mom," I blurt out. *There, take that. Those blinders are coming off.*

"Oh, Chase." She waves me off dismissively.

But I am not deterred. "No, Mom. No, 'oh, Chase'. Those kids are not just hanging out at Cassie's house like you think they are. You need to wake up and see what's happening. You're being duped by your youngest. You have to start keeping a tighter rein on Will."

Mom wrings her hands. She's giving in, allowing herself to see what's right in front of her face. "But Will is only fifteen, Chase," she cries.

"Exactly. He's fifteen, Mom. Not eight."

"He can't be having sex," Mom whispers, stricken.

"He grew up fast," I say gently. "You know that. You're actually lucky he didn't start sooner."

Will is her baby, though, so I know this is difficult for her to hear.

Mom leans back against a work bench, like she needs the support to keep her upright. Maybe she does. She's a leaner, not a supporter.

"I've been a bad mom to you boys," she says in a pained tone.

I don't want to lie, but I don't have it in me to be brutal. I choose to go with a half-truth. "You did the best you could, Mom."

She sometimes did.

We look at each other meaningfully for a few seconds, and then she says, "You don't have to say things that aren't true to try and make me feel better, Chase."

I let out a long, tired breath. "Still, the past is the past. Not much we can do about it now."

My mom touches my forearm. "Honey, I should never have sent you away." She sighs deeply. "You ended up in prison, for God's sake."

"You helped me get out early, though," I offer.

"Small consolation," she snorts.

"Hmm…" I nod.

And then she lays it all out there. "Don't let me off the hook so easily, son. It's time I admit what I did. I gave up on you. I chose the easy way out. Sending you to your grandmother's only made things harder for you. You were already paying for your father's sins and suddenly, there you were, paying for mine." Her eyes fill with tears, and she covers her mouth to stifle a sob. "You reminded me so much of your father back then. I couldn't deal with it. Every time I looked at you, I saw Jack. And seeing your father in you reminded me of how much I had failed him."

Mom chokes back a sob, and I put to words what I accepted today at my father's grave. "You didn't fail him, Mom. None of us did. Dad was fighting his own demons… and he lost."

"But to kill himself," she hisses as she swipes away tears.

I raise a brow. For so many years my mom has maintained that Dad driving off a cliff was an accident. She used to tell me and my brother she believed Dad had been running away that fateful night, that he had taken off so he could start a new life in California.

"You believe it, now?" I ask my mother in a low voice.

"Are you saying you no longer think Dad was running away to start a new life? You finally believe he killed himself?"

"I think I knew it all along," she admits. "I was in so much denial. I just loved him so much. He was my life, Chase, and I didn't want to accept that he could so easily end it all."

My father *was* my mom's life, and, in many ways, she was his. I remember their love well. They were sweet and kind to each other, they loved hard and played hard. No matter what has transpired, I can't deny that Jack and Abby gave me the tools to love like that myself.

My love for Kay is as true and pure as my parents' love once was.

I only hope and pray our love doesn't have a similar tragic ending.

I glance at Mom. She's sobbing softly, wiping away tears. She still feels the pain from all she's lost. All of the money she has nowadays means nothing. Fancy cars, a huge home, the best of everything and still, Mom's as broken as before.

I put my arms around her and give her a heartfelt hug. "Hey, I'm sorry," I whisper. "I'm sorry all this happened to our family."

She holds onto me for dear life. "We were good once, weren't we? The four of us really did have perfect lives. Tell me it wasn't just an illusion, Chase. Tell me it wasn't some image I conjured up in my head by always looking back."

"It was real," I choke out, closing my eyes.

My mom and I hold onto one another, adrift on the choppy seas of our post-destruction lives.

Mom finally speaks first, whispering, "I really messed things up after Jack died, didn't I? I was gone all the time, lost in my own grief." She leans back and looks up at me, sorrow in her big green eyes. "I was never around, Chase. No wonder you turned to drugs."

Shaking my head to let her know not all the fault lies with her, I take a step back and say, "Your absence back then doesn't excuse all the things I did. And, Mom, trust me, I've done far worse things than drugs."

"Do you mean you did some bad things in prison?" she tentatively asks.

"Both in and out," I admit.

It's the truth. I've beaten men, I've used women. I've lied and cheated, and I've stolen things. I'm a would-be drug dealer and a one-time drug user.

And I still deal with temptation every day.

But I am learning.

"You don't do any bad things now, right?" My mom wants to know.

Hearing the hope in her voice is nothing short of heartbreaking, and I think about some of my most recent transgressions—using Missy by letting her blow me behind the Anchor Inn, beating the junkie who hurt Kay, getting drunk and high at Kyle Tanner's, threatening Doug Wilson, keeping secrets from Kay. *Shit*.

I could easily lie to my mother, but what's the point.

"I've done some things recently," I confess. "Things I'm not proud of."

Fear darkens Mom's eyes.

She knows the hold one drug in particular used to have on me. And that is what surely prompts her to ask, "No cocaine, though, right?"

"No cocaine," I assure her.

She visibly relaxes, her shoulders slumping. "Thank God."

She sighs, like the possibility of coke ruling me again might be too much for her to bear.

I hear `ya, I think.

Mom and I are quiet for the next several minutes, lost in our own thoughts. Eventually, she breaks the silence with a laugh.

"What?" I ask.

She points to the top drawer in the work bench. "There are cigarettes in there, and it's taking everything in me not to go over there and light one up. I sure could use a smoke right about now."

I've known all along Abby never quit smoking. But I'm not going to get on her ass now. Not after this talk.

Waving a hand to the workbench, I say, "Go ahead. I won't tell Greg."

She breathes out a sigh of relief. "Thank you, Chase."

While Mom walks over to the workbench and lights up, I point to the motorcycle.

"What about this old thing?" I say. "Where in the hell has it been all this time? I thought we lost everything."

"I thought we did, too," Mom says on an exhale of smoke, her voice pinched with nicotine and tar.

I wave away the smoke and ask, "So, where'd you find the bike?"

I am curious since most everything my family ever owned was lost to bankers, creditors, or pawn shops.

Mom takes another quick hit of her cigarette, and then puts it out on the edge of the work bench. As she's sliding the hardly smoked cig into the pack, she says, "One day, I was cleaning and came across an old shoebox of letters your father had written me. There was a key for a storage unit in the bottom of the box." She shrugs. "Jack must've tucked it in there ages ago and forgot about it. Anyway, the name of the place was on the key, as well as the unit number, so I drove out to the address. That's where I found the bike."

"What else was in the unit?" I ask, curious.

"Nothing. Just the bike."

I look over at the old Indian. "That's pretty amazing we still have it."

"It is," Mom agrees. "And if you want it, Chase, it's yours," she adds with a smile.

I'm thrilled and touched. To have this piece of my dad would mean so much.

I thank my mother, and then say, "Guess Kay and I can drive back on this. We could actually *see* the country, instead of flying over it at thirty thousand feet."

"It's up to you," my mother says. "I can just ship it to Harmony Creek if you change your mind."

"We'll see," I say. "I'll ask Kay what she wants to do."

Mom nods, and then quietly says, "By the way, Chase, I like Kay. She seems like a very nice young lady, perfect for you."

"She *is* perfect for me," I agree.

"Well," Mom continues, "if it's okay with you, I'd like to get to know her a little better. Since she'll be in town all week, would you mind if I ask her out to lunch?"

"I'm fine with that," I say, since I am. "And maybe while you two are out to lunch, I can finally find some alone time with Will."

Mom's expression turns grim, "About Will," she begins. "I'm sorry I pushed him on you this summer. Greg and I should never have gone on that cruise." She shakes her head. "I don't know what I was thinking."

Since I have Mom right where I want her—focused back on being a mother to my brother—I say, "Will needs more structure, Mom. He's struggling. He needs some rules and an anchor to ground him. He needs someone to make him feel safe."

With despair I've never heard from my mom, she says, "You mean he needs *me*."

I sigh. "Yes, Mom, he needs you."

We discuss Will for the next hour. Before we wrap up,

Mom agrees to get him some counseling.

"Is he still doing drugs?" she asks.

I tell her the truth. "He used in Ohio, yes. But toward the end of his stay, he was sober every day."

"Do you think he's an addict?" Mom's voice is a mere whisper, shaky and ragged. She fears my brother will end up in the same place I landed four years ago.

"I don't think he's there yet," I assure her.

Mom blows out a relieved breath. "Thank God."

"Hey," I say sharply. "You still need to get him to talk to someone. Will's not out of the woods yet. You and Greg have to set some rules, get him some help."

"I know," Mom says. "I promise I'll get Will the help he needs."

We talk some more. Talk, not argue. And for the first time in a long time it feels like my mother and I are on the same page.

Maybe, just maybe, with Mom and I working together, there's hope for Will.

EIGHT

Kay

I'M sound asleep, dreaming of Chase. More specifically, I'm dreaming of Chase touching me.

"Mmm," I murmur.

"Kay," he whispers huskily. "Wake up, baby."

I do wake, emerging from a fog of slumber to find Chase undressing me. He is slipping my long sleeping tee over my head, tugging my panties down my legs.

I try to help, but he stills my hands. "Let me," he says.

I nod, and when he has me how he wants me—completely unclothed—his hands ply at my breasts, before slowly trailing down my body.

"So sexy," he whispers as he traces the curve of my waist with his fingertips.

Chase is already naked and glorious. Biting my lip, I soak in the breadth of his shoulders, the tapering *V* of his torso...and the hard length that awaits me.

"Take me," I whisper, desperate for his love.

Chase is instantly over me, above me. He trails kisses down to my sex, where he hungrily laves my folds with his tongue. I grind and moan while he licks and laps, and when I'm just about *there*, he moves up and slides into me.

I come undone, panting, "Chase... Oh, Chase."

In my euphoria, I am wanton. I moan louder than usual, thankful Abby and Greg's bedroom is on the first floor, well out of earshot. Thus unrestrained, I writhe and lift my hips, encouraging Chase to take me in whichever way he desires.

But instead of plunging into me, he withdraws and holds my hips still.

"What?" I ask.

Chase doesn't reply...he just stares at me with those penetrating blue eyes. And when I can't move at all—I am at his mercy—he eases himself back into me.

"Oh," I gasp as he moves in and out of me languidly, lovingly.

"Good?" he whisper-asks.

"Amazing," I reply.

As he continues to make love to me, I moan, "God, you're going to kill me, Chase."

"How's that?" he asks, chuckling as his lips brush over mine.

Against his mouth, I murmur, "Because you make me want to give you more and more. There's never an end to my desire to please you. I want to give you all of me."

He gives me a little more of his weight, and I spread my legs a little more to accommodate him.

"That's good, Kay." he rasps. "Since what I want is *all* of you."

I open myself to Chase, and I give him everything I have—my heart, my body, my soul. I feel him taking a piece of me with every slow, savoring thrust. But for everything Chase takes, he gives back twice as much.

"I love you, Kay," he murmurs in my ear. "I love you so much."

As he pours his love into me, I think of the conversation we had back in Ohio, the one about having a baby. I wasn't ready then, but I feel more than ready now. I have a few more weeks of active birth control, and then that's it. I am definitely not getting another Depo shot in September. Chase will be happy with my decision. He wants a baby, and I am finally completely ready to give him one.

Later, wrapped up in Chase's strong arms, but before sleep has found either of us, I ask him, "Do you still want to marry me?"

"Are you kidding?" he replies, chuckling softly. Pulling me close to him, he kisses the top of my head. "I'll marry you right now, baby, if that's what you want. We *are* in Las Vegas, after all. The chapels are open twenty-four-seven."

Whoa, I hadn't thought of that.

But now that's it's out there...

"Hmm," I muse aloud. "Father Maridale would kill us, though, if we were to get married here in Vegas."

Chase counters with, "We could always get married a second time in the church back home."

I prop up on one elbow and stare down at this crazy man who might really be thinking we should do this. "You're not serious, are you?"

"About the church wedding?" he asks. "Or about the getting married tonight?"

"Both."

His eyes meet mine. "Oh, I'm serious, Kay. I'm going to love you forever no matter what. So, I say let's make it official in the eyes of the law. In fact, I think we *should* do it tonight."

I can't think of a single reason not to marry Chase as

soon as possible, so I say, "Yes, let's do it."

And then I am showering Chase in a flurry of kisses. My joy is uncontained, and I'm bursting with emotion. I could lie here forever with my man. But we must make ourselves get out of bed, especially when Chase informs me, "The Clark County Marriage License Bureau is only open till midnight."

"Better hurry, then," I say as I playfully jump up and scamper to the bathroom. Chase catches up to me. He lifts me into his arms and carries me the rest of the way.

Minutes later, we are showering together. Chase tenderly washes my body, but when his fingers linger a bit too long at my softest spots, I remind him, "We have a wedding to attend, right?"

"We sure do," he replies, smiling brightly.

Luckily, Chase packed a suit — black — for the possibility he'd have to wear it for something out here in Las Vegas. He tells me, "I originally thought Mom and Greg would plan some fancy dinner out on the town."

He leans down to kiss me while I finish with my makeup in front of the dresser mirror. "But this is a much better reason to get dressed up."

"For sure," I reply, giggling as Chase plants tiny kisses down my neck, his gentle nips tickling at my tender skin.

"Okay, back to getting ready," he announces as her steps away from the dresser.

But still, he remains close, watching me as he fiddles with a set of cufflinks. When I glance up at him in the reflection of the mirror, I can't believe how incredibly handsome he is dressed in a suit and tie.

Reluctantly, I turn away so I can slip a white eyelet lace dress over my head.

I think of how much Chase loves the dress I've chosen to wear. It is the same dress I had on the day he stole my hair tie, the tie he placed back in my hair so gently that day.

There are no hair ties going in my hair tonight, but Chase does insist on brushing out my chestnut mane. Careful, so carefully, his brush strokes feel divine. Tonight, Chase touches me like I might break.

"I can't believe you really want to become my wife," he whispers, leaning into me, his chest pressing to my back.

I slowly turn to face him, and lower his hand with the brush to his side.

"I want to marry you, Chase. More than you can imagine. In fact, there's nothing more I'd rather do."

He smiles and touches my face. With everything I am feeling in this moment, I begin to slowly recite lines I memorized long ago, lines I promised myself I'd know by heart for the day I wedded the love of my life.

And today is that day.

"I, Kay Stanton," I softly murmur, "…take you, Chase Gartner, to be my lawful wedded husband. To have and to hold from this day forward, for better or for worse…"

Chase picks up where I leave off. "… For richer, for poorer, in sickness and in health, to love and to cherish…"

Together we say, "From this day forward, until death do us part."

Two hours later, we are reciting the exact same vows once more.

Only this time it's for real.

Chase and I have opted for a ceremony at a chapel in one of the nicer Vegas hotels. We even stopped by a twenty-four hour jewelry store in the arcade shops beforehand so we could purchase two simple gold bands.

And now we are here, doing this, getting married in a quaint little wedding chapel. We are surrounded by mountains of flowers left over from a previous ceremony. It's so pretty in here. Amethyst-toned stained glass windows sparkle and reflect the glow of all the lit candles in the small room. And though there are few people in the pews—just the two hotel employees bearing witness—this feels right.

Chase and I have been on our own for a long time now.

Sure, we're healing old wounds and reconnecting with family, but when you get right down to it, Chase and I only really have one another to rely on.

So, yes, we'll have a church wedding when we return home, but that one will be for everyone else.

This one—today, now—this one is for us.

"I now pronounce you husband and wife," the officiant announces.

And then it's done.

"We're married," I say to Chase.

"Yes, we're married, sweet girl," he whispers as his lips brush over mine.

We hear, "You may kiss the bride," and we kiss...and kiss...and kiss.

After the ceremony, we stop by the hotel casino to celebrate. We play some slots, and I win a little money, which is helpful since we just blew a bunch on the rings and ceremony.

On the way home, Chase stops by an all-night liquor store and buys a bottle of good champagne. And back at the house, the fates smile down on us, allowing us to find a single wedge of brie in the refrigerator.

"It's a sign," I say to Chase.

He slips the package of soft cheese from my grasp and places it on the counter. "I think you may be right," he says.

And then, when he begins to search the cabinets for something to spread the brie on, he distractedly adds, "Though I wonder what kind of sign it could be. A sign that the fates sensed we were hungry? A sign my mom likes the same cheese as us?"

He's totally messing with me, so I smack his arm. "It's a sign tonight was meant to be, silly man."

"I know," he laughs.

In a much more serious tone, I add, "We did the right thing by getting married tonight, Chase."

"I couldn't agree more," he replies.

Finding a package of crackers, at last, he sets them aside.

Turning fully to me, he tells me, "This is one of the best days of my life."

My eyes tear up as I reply, "Me, too."

And then, out of curiosity, I ask, "What are the others?"

"Best days of my life?"

"Yes."

Touching my cheek, he says, "I could list them, but let's just say every single one involves you, Kay."

"Chase…"

Before things turn too emotional in the middle of the kitchen, Chase grabs the crackers, cheese, and champagne and says, "How about we go upstairs and make this one of the best *nights* of our lives, my lovely wife?"

His blues dance mischievously, and I know we won't be eating brie spread on crackers—nor drinking champagne—for very long.

I sweep my hand out in front of me and say, "Lead the way, dear husband."

NINE

Chase

KAY and I make our first decision as man and wife the next morning. After sleeping in—and making love for the umpteenth time—we decide to keep our marriage a secret, for now. After we tuck our rings in our suitcases, we shower and get ready for the day ahead.

When we finally venture downstairs, we find my mother in the kitchen, where she eyes us curiously.

"Hmm," she says after a beat. "You two sure were sleepyheads. It's nearly noon."

I roll my eyes and grab a carton of orange juice from the refrigerator. "Yep, we were tired," I mutter.

Mom's not done yet, though. She rests her hip against the granite-top island in the center of the room, and says, "I imagine so, seeing you two were out so late last night."

I know Mom didn't hear us leave the house or return, as we were extra quiet.

Seeing my confused expression, she says, "I noticed

the rental car was moved."

"Aah," I remark.

Mom's still not satisfied. Tapping one manicured fingernail on the counter, she says, "I also noticed my brie is missing from the refrigerator. And two champagne flutes are gone from the china closet." She raises an eyebrow. "Were we perhaps celebrating something?"

Mom would flip if she knew Kay and I got married last night. Kay suspects my mom will have this reaction, as well, so the poor girl quickly hides her sure-to-give-us-away expression by raising her glass of juice to her mouth.

"Sweet girl," I mutter, chuckling. "Don't worry. I got this."

Turning to my mother, I say, "Kay and I were just having a little bubbly and some cheese to celebrate this being her first time in Las Vegas."

"Oh, really?" Mom replies, skepticism coloring her tone.

"Yes, really," I retort dryly.

I have no intention of divulging that Kay and I got married last night. Abby is going to have a coronary as it is when she discovers we did things the way we did. She's all about big weddings and lots of fanfare. But really, our way was the best for us. This love I share with Kay is so personal that I don't really care to have a crowd of people there to witness all our raw emotions.

Of course, I'll have to get over that issue before the church wedding. Hopefully, I can delay that event for as long as possible.

Just then—and fortuitously saving all of us from any further discussion about last night—Will waltzes in.

"Hey, guys," he says nonchalantly as he grabs the OJ. "What's up?"

"Not much," Mom replies. "How was your time at Cassie's?"

Before Will can answer, I cough. "I bet you two crazy kids had *lots* of fun."

My tone is full of suggestion, and Will shoots me a did-you-have-to-go-there look.

"Dude," he says.

I'm not trying to be a dick to my brother, so I throw him an apologetic smile. My intent is for my mother to stop treating him like he's ten years old. Mom also catches sight of my gaze, and her eyes grow soft and wounded.

Shit, she wants me to give her a chance to do the right thing. *Okay, okay*, I think as I give her a look that conveys I'm about to back off.

With the momentary rough spot behind us, Mom directs her attention to Kay. "Honey," she says to my girl, "would you like to come to lunch with me tomorrow afternoon? It would give us some time to talk, and I was just telling Chase that I think we should get to know each other better."

"Uhh…" Kay looks to me for guidance, but I just shrug. This decision is totally up to her.

When Kay sees I don't care either way, she tells my mom, "Yeah, okay. Sounds like fun."

Turning to me, Will interjects, "Hey, Chase, since Kay will be out with Mom, do you want to do something tomorrow, just us?"

I wait for Mom to chime in with, "Oh, aren't you going to include Greg," but then I am informed that Greg is leaving late tonight for a three-week business trip in Phoenix.

Sigh of relief. Hate to say it, but I'm kind of glad he won't be around the house. Greg is a nice enough guy, sure, but he's too hands-off in the parenting department.

"I'm sure we'll find something fun to do," I say to Will, and then, because I know it gets him all worked up, I reach over and ruffle his dark-blond hair.

Will swats me away. "God, you are such a freak," he mutters.

But really, he likes the big-brother attention.

The remainder of Sunday is uneventful; we all just laze around the house. In the evening, Mom announces she wants us all to watch a movie in the family room.

"Before Greg has to leave," she says, eyeing me with hope in her gaze.

Sorry, Mom, I think before I decline the invitation. Movie nights used to be a big thing for me, my mom, and my dad, but that was like a fucking thousand years ago. Greg is not Dad, and I won't pretend he is.

Mom is disappointed, but she gets over it quickly enough. Especially when Sunday rolls into Monday and noontime arrives. It's lunchtime for the girls, and let's just say Mom is chomping at the bit to get rolling.

"Kay, are you ready?" she calls out loudly from the hallway as she's knocking on our closed bedroom door.

I roll my eyes and try to catch Kay's gaze from where I'm seated, leaned back against the headboard. My wife, though, is too busy in front of the mirror, adjusting her cute, floral strapless dress. She pays me no heed.

Hmm, I know what will get her attention...

"Good thing I don't have you bent over that dresser," I say in a low, suggestive tone.

"Chase!" Kay motions to the closed door. "Hush, before your mom hears you."

"Like I care," I scoff.

Mom knocks again, and this time Kay steps away from the dresser and opens the door.

"I'm ready," she announces brightly to Mom, who peeks in nosily.

I give my mother a wave from my spot on the bed. Thank God Kay and I actually decided to make the bed earlier. It was a wreck from a torrid morning, and I wouldn't have wanted the sight to scar Mom for life.

"Will is waiting downstairs for you," my mother reminds me. "He wants to know what you have planned for the two of you this afternoon."

Translation: Mom wants to know.

"Yeah, okay. He'll find out soon enough." I reply, giving away no details of my plans with Will.

I actually do have a plan—I'm taking Will out on the motorcycle. I plan to head to the desert this afternoon, the more desolate parts. I'm going to do what my dad did for me, teach my brother how to drive the old Indian. It's not completely legal since Will has no driver's permit, but it's how Dad taught me. Besides, I did a little research and found that Will can apply for a learner's permit at fifteen and a half, which, for him, is just a couple months away.

And, to be honest, I'd rather teach Will than have someone like Greg try to do it.

Blood is thicker than water, and all that jazz.

Kay gets Mom moving, giving me a little good-bye wave when they are halfway out the door. I'm not having any of that crap, though. I stand and go to Kay, where I wrap my arms around her and kiss her good and properly.

When I involve tongue, Mom clears her throat. "Chase, really," she murmurs, shaking her head.

Sometimes it is entirely too much fun to push Mom's buttons. But since she looks so put-out with me, I decide to throw her a bone.

Draping my arm loosely around her shoulders, I squeeze lightly. "Have fun, Mom. And take good care of my girl."

Abby is beside herself with the attention I'm lavishing on her. It's not much, but I don't often show her any real affection, since we're usually too busy butting heads.

Kay smiles and mouths, "I'm proud of you" when Mom turns her back and starts to walk away.

"Better get going," I reply softly.

After they're out of sight, I return to the bedroom.

This trip is turning out better than expected. First, I sure as hell didn't think I'd become Kay's husband two days in. How crazy is that? This trip has been good in other ways, too. I feel like the visit to my father's grave has given me some inner peace. Plus, Mom and I are finally reaching a better place, better than where we've been in years.

Will yells up the stairs, breaking me out of my thoughts. "Chase, dude, what's taking you so long? Are we going or not?"

"Yeah," I yell back. "I'll be down in a sec."

I start down the stairs, thinking how Will is my last hurdle. If I can keep him on track, I'll count this trip to Nevada as a raging success.

And maybe then Kay and I can finally head back to Ohio and get started on the rest of our lives.

TEN

Kay

"CAN I tell you something, Kay?" Chase's mother's voice is a mere whisper as she leans across the table, lending an air of seriousness to what has thus far been nothing but light lunchtime conversation. Dishes were cleared minutes ago by the waiter, and we've just started to work on dessert.

Well, *I'm* working on dessert. Abby is busy working on her third glass of wine.

"Sure," I respond as I hack off a good-sized portion of the cheesecake in front of me.

Abby takes a long sip from her glass of wine, and then gestures for the waiter to bring her another.

"I didn't want to say anything to Chase," she begins as she sets down her glass. "But I really feel I must tell someone."

"Okay," I reply slowly, hoping Abby knows that whatever she tells me will be reported back to Chase.

Sighing and rubbing at an invisible wrinkle in the tablecloth, she says, "Greg was upset with Will before he left the other day. Very upset."

"Oh." I push my cheesecake away, my appetite dampened. "Why was he mad? What happened?"

My pulse is racing. There are so many possibilities. Did Greg find drugs in Will's possession? Did Will once again steal from Greg's liquor cabinet? Or maybe this is an issue involving Cassie.

But my biggest question is why has it taken Abby all week to bring this up? It's Thursday and our third lunch date this week. There have been multiple opportunities for her to bring up this subject.

The waiter arrives, and Abby drains her new glass of wine in record time. She places it on the table then levels me with grim, green eyes. "Greg owns a few collector guns," she says, "like Old West stuff." She waves her hand around dismissively. "Anyway, that's not important. What's important is that one gun is missing, and Greg is convinced Will stole it."

Oh, no. My heart is hammering in my chest.

"Why would Greg think such a thing?" I ask in a voice far calmer than I feel. "What would Will do with some old collector gun, anyway?"

"Probably sell it for drug money," Abby states resignedly.

Oh, but I know better.

After Abby orders yet another glass of wine, she goes off on a tangent of how she plans to follow through on her promise to Chase.

"I need to get Will into counseling," she says. "I'm going to work on that soon, too. I have some numbers already. I got them from a friend. I'll make some calls later." *Blah, blah, blah.*

I nod, but really I am hearing nothing. Running through

my head, drowning out Abby, are my own thoughts. Thoughts that revolve around the fact I know Greg is absolutely correct—Will stole the collector gun. And *that* gun is the one Will gave to Chase, pretending all along that it was the firearm he bought from Kyle.

Yeah, right. No wonder Chase was suspicious. He suspected his brother deceived him, and he was right. Will lied. That is why he gave up the gun so easily. Giving up the collector gun appeased Chase, who, despite his continued reservations, always hopes for the best from his brother.

But the biggest concern is that Will has a gun in his possession…still.

Damn. I knew things were sailing along far too smoothly. I knew this much goodness couldn't last. All week Chase has been spending time with his brother, building bonds that were long ago broken.

Has it all been a lie? Was Will just appeasing Chase in order to keep him from the truth? If so, that will kill poor Chase.

"We need to go," I suddenly announce, my fork clattering to the plate.

"What?" Abby is clearly perplexed by my urgent tone, her green eyes questioning. "Why?" she says. "Do we have somewhere we need to be?"

"Yes." I push back my chair and signal the waiter for the check.

Chase and Will are out in the desert today, just as they've been every other day this week. Chase has been taking Will to the same desolate roads his father once took him to. He's trying to teach Will how to safely and properly operate a motorcycle. Every morning, I watch them ride away on the same bike Jack Gartner long ago taught his eldest to ride years before.

But is the bond between Chase and Will as strong as

Chase believes?

I don't know. Because much like Jack Gartner during his last days on Earth, it appears his youngest son has inherited the same gene that leans toward deception.

The waiter brings the bill, and I hastily throw enough money on the table to cover my and Abby's portion of the check, plus a big tip.

"Wait, I'll get that," Abby says, trying to stop me.

"No." I stand. "Let's just go."

When Abby stands up she's a little shaky from the wine, making me glad I drove today. I sure wouldn't want to get into a heated debate with Abby over the wisdom of operating an automobile, not after all the wine she's consumed.

On our way to the car, I take out my cell and text Chase: *I really need to talk with you ASAP. It's urgent.*

I receive no response, not that I expect one. Chase and Will are out in an area with limited cell coverage, a mostly untouched region of the desert.

I, however, am quickly reminded that I am in a very "touched" region of the desert when I head home and end up in snarled freeway traffic.

"Oh, great," I mutter.

I feel Abby's eyes on me. She's sobering up. "Kay," she says slowly and deliberately. "Are you going to tell me what's going on? If it's about Will, I deserve to know. I *am* his mother, after all."

"I know," I quietly respond.

And, yes, she is his mother, but I fear her reaction when I tell her what's really going on.

So, for now, I choose to say nothing. The silence in the car becomes deafening, though, particularly since the traffic is barely moving.

"At this rate," I murmur in an attempt to make conversation, "it will take us an hour to get to the house."

"Hmm," Abby says, clearly unhappy I'm not giving her the deets on what's up with Will.

Can I stave her off for an hour? I wonder.

Unlikely, I determine.

So, under the hot Nevada sun—the same sun that is shining somewhere on Chase and Will—I inform Abby of all that has been happening.

I begin with the events that occurred in Ohio. I tell her how Will made friends with a local kid named Jared. I detail his subsequent slip-ups with drugs, especially when Cassie's stepdad started harassing her again.

Finally, with a sigh, I get to the part about Will buying a gun.

While I'm finishing my tale, Abby stares down at her hands, folded so neatly in her lap.

"Chase should have told me all this," she whispers when I'm done.

Despite her surprisingly calm demeanor, I don't have the heart to tell her Chase didn't think she could handle this information.

But she knows. She knows despite my holding back. She's well-aware of what Chase thinks of her parenting skills.

Abby shakes her head once, twice. Then she wrings her hands. Finally, she proves Chase was right not to tell her about Will when she says, "Oh, Kay, in times like these I just wish Jack were still alive. He'd know what to say to Will, what to do to help him. This is just too much for me to handle."

"Don't worry; Chase is handling it," I reply dryly.

"He shouldn't have to," she mumbles under her breath.

Whoa, I'm shocked.

"I don't disagree," I whisper.

That remark earns me a surprised glance from Abby, as well as a harrumph.

I'm quick to add, "Chase is probably the only one who can really handle Will."

Abby nods. "Yeah, you're probably right."

She turns away and peers out the side window. Clearly, she knows her limitations.

After inching through the last of the backed-up traffic, the road finally opens up. It is smooth sailing from that point on, and we make it back to the house in good time.

As we turn into the gated community, a quick glance at the clock in the dash informs me that it's almost four o'clock.

Abby says what I'm thinking at that moment: "Wonder if Chase and Will are home yet."

"I was thinking the same thing," I reply with a laugh.

We let out simultaneous exhales when, seconds later, we pull to the front of the house and see the motorcycle is parked off to the side.

"They're here," I say, relief in my tone.

"Thank God," Abby whispers.

Our shared respite is short-lived, though, as we walk through the front door.

Chase is in the entry hall, placing his helmet on a table by the far wall. It's obvious he's only been home for a short while—minutes, maybe. It is also abundantly clear there is no one with him.

"Where's Will?" Abby asks, glancing around.

She rushes over to Chase, and his eyes follow her hand as she grabs hold of his forearm.

His gaze slides to me, and he asks, "What's going on? What's wrong?"

Though Chase's question is directed to me, Abby answers. And when she starts speaking, she breaks down.

"Oh, Chase," she sobs, tears flowing. "I know about the gun. I know about the trouble you had with Will in Ohio. I'm so sorry for that. But it's good I know everything. I should know."

"How do you know," Chase asks slowly.

"Kay told me," Abby replies.

I cringe as Chase's gaze falls on me sharply.

"Sorry," I mouth. He shakes his head, and I add more firmly, "I had to tell her, Chase."

I want to say more. I want to tell him I wouldn't have made a decision like that without talking it over with him first. But under the circumstances, what choice did I have?

His eyes, a troubled blue, remain on me. "What else is going on?" he says. "I can tell there's more."

"There is," I confirm. And after a deep breath to calm my frazzled nerves, I say, "Will didn't give you the gun he bought from Kyle. You were right to be suspicious. Turns out, he gave you a gun he stole from Greg."

Chase suspected as much, and I just confirmed it. But I can't read his emotions, not today, not like how I normally do.

"I see," he says slowly, giving away nothing.

I go to Chase. Something is off. "What's wrong?" I ask.

"Where's Will?" Abby interjects.

Chase—so very tall as he towers over the two women in his life—looks down at his mother, and then at me.

Grimly, he says, "We may have an even bigger problem."

"What?" his mother and I ask at the same time.

Chase sighs. "I just dropped Will off at the last place I ever would have taken him had I known what you just told me."

His mother—still so clueless—asks, "Where? Where did you take him?"

I provide the answer Chase appears too frustrated to say.

"Chase dropped Will off at Cassie's house," I say.

ELEVEN

Chase

Fuck. I've been duped by my fifteen-year-old little shit of a brother. Should I really be surprised? I mean, hell, I suspected the gun he gave me the other night was not the firearm he bought from Kyle Tanner. But, still, I can't believe Will would put on a charade all week, acting as if everything is fine.

That's exactly what he's done, though.

I've asked him numerous times how things have been going, and every single fucking time that kid has told me everything was cool.

I've heard statements such as: "Cassie hasn't heard from Paul. He must've skipped town."

Or when I asked him about how he's been faring, his response was this: "I'm doing great, Chase." Coupled with a, "I feel really good, bro. Never been better."

And then there was this gem from earlier today…

Will and I were eating sandwiches we made this

morning before taking off for the desert. Under the desert heat, and after taking a bite, Will swallowed, and said, "Hey, thank you for bringing me out here, Chase." He motioned to the bike, to the surrounding desert. "This place is pretty cool. And this week has been awesome."

It was that last bit, said with such sincerity, that prompted me to say, "Okay, sure," when Will then asked if I could drop him off at Cassie's house on the way home.

"Just for a couple of hours," he added, like he was the most reasonable teenager ever.

"Her mother will be there, right?" I asked, suspicious of his true motives, but wanting so badly to give him a chance.

"Not when you drop me off," Will replied, his face the portrait of honesty. "But she'll be home right after. She usually comes in from work around four."

I respected his truthfulness, or what I thought was the truth.

What a joke. It's slightly past four now, and I have a strong suspicion Mrs. Sutter still isn't home. Come to think of it, she's probably on a business trip somewhere and won't be home at all today.

Shit, this is my fault. Why do I continue to trust Will so implicitly?

Sighing, I know the answer—I'm blinded by my love for my brother. I want to believe Will is honest and trustworthy.

But he's not.

My mother takes a step back, her hand dropping from my arm, but Kay remains by my side. Yeah, my wife has my back.

"Didn't you get my text?" she murmurs.

"No, I haven't checked my phone for hours."

"It doesn't matter now," Kay says, waving her hand dismissively. "I was hoping to warn you ahead of time, but it's too late."

"Yeah," I mumble. "Warn me of Will's lies, built on Cassie's secrets, huh?"

My eyes lock in on Kay's caramels, filled with understanding. She's well-aware of how sick to death I am of Will's lies and secrets. In fact, I'm sick of deception all the way around, making me half-tempted to divulge to my mother — right here, right now — that Kay and I are married.

Kay, reading my intent so well, shakes her head, and whispers, "Not now, Chase."

Discreetly, she glances at my mother, as do I.

Mom is pacing, trying to keep herself together. Kay's right; now is definitely not the time to announce to my bereft mother I got married right under her nose and failed to include her in any way, shape, or form.

"Yeah, you're right," I say softly to Kay.

She and I can deal with only so much fallout at a time, and my brother has provided more than enough shit to wade through right now.

"So, what should we do?" my mother asks, suddenly turning to us.

Her eyes beseech mine, like I have all the answers. *I wish, Mom, I wish.*

I may not have all the answers, but I do have one. "I think I should head back over to Cassie's. If Will is there, I'll bring him back. And," I add, deadly serious, "I am getting that gun out of his possession."

Kay immediately offers, "I'll go with you."

I nod an assent while Mom bites her lip and frowns.

"Maybe I should go, too," she murmurs.

"No!" Kay and I simultaneously reply.

All I need is for my hysterical mom to make things worse. Kay knows this, as well.

My mother's face falls, and I say in a placating voice,

"Look, Mom... Someone has to stay here. You know, in case Will is out with Cassie and she drops him off or something."

It's bullshit. Will's not coming home. Not without some forceful encouragement. But Mom plays along and pretends to agree. "Yeah, you're right, Chase. I'll stay here." Her tone is flat. She's given up already.

And that is how we leave my mother—in the entry hall, wanting to be a good mother but not knowing how.

For as much as some things change, other things remain the same.

Out by the rental car, Kay stops me. Her arms go around me, comforting. She stands on her tiptoes and kisses my lips.

When she lowers herself to her diminutive size, she looks up at me, and says, "I love you, Chase."

I reach out and caress her cheek with my knuckles. "I love you too, babe."

I need this woman, always.

Fifteen minutes later, we are knocking on Cassie's front door. There's no sign of Mrs. Sutter's car in the driveway. *Home from work by four, my ass.* The other thing I find odd is Cassie's car is not here either.

Hmm...

I glance at Kay and find her staring over at the empty driveway, same as me.

"Maybe they went somewhere," she offers.

"Yeah, maybe," I respond. I sound unconvincing, even to my own ears.

Just then the front door swings open. Cassie, looking quite unlike how I've ever seen her before today, wavers uncertainly. She stares at us with heavy-lidded eyes. All she's wearing is a long tee with boy shorts.

It's pretty obvious to me the girl is fucked up.

"Guys," she slurs, giggling. "Come on in." She steps

aside and makes a sweeping motion with her arm before almost toppling over. "Oops," she says, laughing.

Kay grabs hold of Cassie's arm to steady her as we step into the house. "Where's your mother?" she asks.

Cassie leans forward, directing her answer to me, not Kay. I get a good whiff of alcohol as she lazily breathes out, "Not here, obviously."

"Clearly," I murmur. And then, in a firmer voice, I inquire, "Where is Will?"

Cassie dances out of Kay's grasp, ignoring my question. She spins in a little circle, singing, "Will, Will, Will. Oh, I love my beautiful boy."

Kay looks at me and shakes her head. "What's she on?"

"Jesus, I have no idea," I reply. "She's drunk, but maybe she took some pills, too."

Cassie stumbles down two steps leading to a sunken living room with Kay and me following closely behind. It's dimly lit in the living room, as all the blinds are drawn. There are empty liquor bottles strewn across the floor… among other things.

I pick up a couple of these items — a pill bottle belonging to Cassie's mom, Cassie's discarded jeans, a foil wrapper. All pieces to a puzzle that give me a story: Will and Cassie drank, took a few pills, and had sex.

Cassie picks up a bottle of booze and takes off the cap.

"Whoa, hold up there." I swipe the bottle from her grasp. "I think you've had enough." Handing her the pair of jeans still in my other hand, I say, "Here, put on some clothes."

I get no argument. Cassie is not like Will. But when she tries to put on her jeans, she falls back on the couch.

Kay hurries over to help her. "What happened after Chase dropped Will off earlier?" she asks Cassie as she helps her into her jeans. "And where is Will now?"

"He left," Cassie replies flatly. "He got in my car and

took off."

Fully dressed now, she leans back into the cushions and flings her hand out to add emphasis to the "took off" portion of her remark.

I sit down next to Cassie.

"Where did he go?" I ask. "And please tell me he wasn't as fucked up as you are right now when he got behind the wheel of that car."

"He drank a little," Cassie admits. "But he didn't take any of the pills. He said he needed to be thinking straight."

Despite her own less-than-coherent state, Cassie has yet to divulge *where* my brother has gone.

The girl is stalling, so, again, I ask, "Where exactly did Will go, Cassie?"

Cassie twirls a lock of flaxen hair around her index finger. Studying it, she says softly, "He went to take care of Paul."

And that is when I lose it.

Turning to this far-too-nonchalant girl, I grind out, "What the fuck does that mean? Where is my brother? And what the hell is he up to now?"

My tone is harsh, and Cassie winces. But she also wisely answers.

"We found out where Paul has been staying," she says quietly. "Well, I found out. He called here. Paul, that is. He said he needed to talk to my mom. I knew it was a farce, though. I knew he was calling to talk to me."

"What'd you say to him?" I ask.

"I talked to him for a while. And then I had an idea, a plan to trap him. I tricked him into thinking I wanted to meet up with him." She shudders. "Anyway, my ploy worked. He told me where he's been staying.

"And that's where Will is now," I finish for her.

"Yes, that's where Will is heading. But Paul thinks *I'm* driving out to meet him. That's why Will had to use my car. He doesn't want to tip Paul off since he has to get close enough to —"

"Are you fucking crazy?" I yell, cutting her off.

Cassie scoots away and cowers to Kay.

That does nothing to deter me as I continue, unabated, "Why would you let my brother go meet up with that fucking animal? You *do* realize you could get him in serious trouble, right?"

I am livid. I know Will makes his own decisions, but I can't help but feel Cassie is primarily at fault. This girl fosters Will's protective side, but she also takes advantage of it.

"Why didn't you just call the police?" Kay softly asks Cassie.

Kay is far calmer than I.

"If you knew where Paul was," she continues, "why didn't you call and tell the authorities? There's a restraining order out on Paul. The police could have taken him in."

"We could call them now," Cassie offers.

"Too little, too late," I mutter.

"Why?" Cassie asks.

"You just sent my brother to Paul's place with a fucking gun in his possession. Do you want the police to show up and arrest Will?"

I'm riled, still, and Kay shoots me a look indicating I should calm the fuck down.

"Chase," she mutters, "please."

"I want Paul gone," Cassie whimpers. "That's all."

"You want Paul gone," I echo, shaking my head. "And my brother is supposed to be the one to get rid of him for you, huh? That's just great."

There's so much more I long to say. Things like: what about my brother's safety and well-being? Would you have him ruin his entire life for you?

But the answer to all my questions is clear in Cassie's

actions. She may claim she loves Will, but she doesn't know what love is. If she did, she wouldn't put Will in this kind of jeopardy.

With Kay's influence, I finally manage to calm down. She and I eventually obtain the information we need from Cassie. We learn Paul has been staying in a trailer out on a road aptly named Vulture Mine Road.

"I know the area," I mumble under my breath.

And I do, quite well. Ironically, Vulture Mine Road is not far from where Will and I have been hanging all week with the bike. That whole area is nothing but hardcore desert, pure wilderness, a good hiding place for the likes of Paul.

Before Kay and I leave to go retrieve Will, Cassie tells Kay she's feeling sick. "Can you help me to the bathroom?" she asks meekly.

"Of course," Kay replies.

She gives me a look, and I shrug. "It'll just be a few extra minutes," she whispers.

"Sure, okay."

With Kay and Cassie out of the living room, I decide to do a little cleaning up. Truth is, I have to do something, or I'll fucking crack.

I start by dumping all the alcohol down the kitchen sink. Then I work on the rest of the junk. The pill bottle— some kind of pain medication—appears empty, so I throw it away, along with the condom wrapper.

Sighing, I try to look on the bright side. At least Will's been safe with Cassie.

Still, if she were to get pregnant... *Jesus*. I can't even fathom such a thought.

When Kay returns to the living room, alone, I ask her, "Where's Cassie?"

"She's lying down in her room."

"Maybe you should stay here with her," I suggest.

If at all possible, my preference would be for Kay to remain here. I'd like to keep her as far from danger as possible.

But from the look on her face, I see my stubborn girl's not having any of my good, logical reasoning.

"Chase," she says, her voice tired but firm. "Please don't fight me on this. I'm going with you. We already decided that that is the plan."

I put up my hands. "Okay, okay. If that's what you really want."

"It *is* what I want." She sighs. "You're not doing this alone."

"Fine," I say, acquiescing. "There is a condition, though."

I eye her intently, until she says, "What?"

"You are absolutely not coming up to that trailer with me. I'll park down the road, before we reach the place. I want you to wait in the car while I check things out, okay?"

On this, I am not budging, so it's good when Kay replies, "Yes, yes, okay. Wait in the car. I got it."

I pray she does, in fact, 'get it,' because the last thing I need is for Kay to accidentally get shot by my misguided, gun-toting brother.

TWELVE

Kay

I DON'T like this plan. I don't like it at all.

As Chase and I make a turn onto the disturbingly named Vulture Mine Road, full darkness descends, turning the mountains to shadowy silhouettes.

The night has an ominous vibe, prompting me to say to Chase, "I have a bad feeling about this."

"Bad feeling or not," he replies, "I have to help my brother."

"I know," I whisper, accepting his decision.

Still, when Chase slows to an almost stop, I place my hand on his arm. "I'm not suggesting you not help Will. I just want you to promise to be extra careful."

Chase is so big and strong and capable, but he *is* just a man. He's not a superhero like the lead character in Will's comic book, the one I know in my heart Will modeled after his older brother.

Chase pulls off the road and the rental car dips down

into a gravel turn-out. After turning off the ignition, he turns to me.

I lean over to him so he can enfold me in his strong arms. "I'll be careful," he assures me.

I'm strong for Chase. I don't let him see any of the tears building in my eyes, even though all I feel like doing is crying in his arms.

After a hug — which lasts a while, but not long enough — Chase pulls away. Slowly, he opens the driver's-side door, allowing the dome light to bathe him in an orangey kind of glow.

His light-brown hair looks slightly coppery, and I reach over and run my fingers through the soft locks. "You have two sides to you, Chase, and I love them both," I softly proclaim.

His eyes go to mine, his blues questioning. "Two sides?" he asks.

"Yes," I reply as I tug gently on the ends of his hair. "Soft," I say, combing through the silky strands. "And hard." My hand moves to the rough stubble on Chase's jaw. "Like this."

I touch his lips, mouthing the word, "Soft."

He smiles.

I laugh.

Lowering my hand, I grasp his solid bicep. "And hard," I nod and raise my eyebrows. "Actually very hard," I add. "Impressive."

This time, Chase is the one to laugh. But he quiets when I skim my hand across his chest and stop at his heart.

"Soft" I whisper, "so very soft."

Chase grabs my hand. "Kay..."

His eyes say everything he doesn't — or cannot — say.

"Go," I tell him, turning away. "Go, before I try and stop you."

I hear him sigh.

I hear him close the door.
And then he's gone.
The outcome of the night now lies in fate's hands.

THIRTEEN

Will

A M *I making a mistake? Is this the right thing to do?*
Truth is, I don't know.
Why does it seem I always have questions, but never any answers?

I know what Chase would say to me. He'd tell me I'm throwing my life away. He's big nowadays on keeping on task. But in the same breath, Chase is always urging me to be courageous.

He says shit like, "Follow your heart, Will. But always try to be a good man."

Well, saving Cassie from Paul seems like something a "good" man would take care of. Right?

In any case, I have no choice. I have to try. See, Cassie doesn't have a father to do things like protect her from crazy perverts. Her dad died several years ago, same as mine. My deal—though rotten—was still better than hers. Better because I have an older brother who'd lay his life down for me.

Cassie has no one but me. That's why I'm manning up. Someone has to take care of this fucked-up situation.

And we need a solution that is permanent.

I drive out to the deep desert, not far from where Chase and I were earlier in the day.

Shit, now that I think on it, this whole week has been great. Riding Dad's old Indian, what a trip that has been. Mom's had that thing in the garage for ages. Greg usually ignores it, but I sometimes catch my mom out there, staring at that bike like it holds some answer she's been looking for. She gets that faraway look in her eyes, the same look she gets anytime she's lost in her memories of my dad.

Dad. I shake my head.

This family. Sometimes, I swear…

I just thank God for Chase. If it wasn't for this thing with Cass hanging over my fucking head, I'd count the past few days spent with my brother as some of the best.

Spending time with Chase was always good. Well, until it wasn't. But it's good again these days, and that's all that counts. It's a relief, a lifting of a burden. I spent too many years of my young life harboring a lot of resentment towards my older brother. I hated that he'd turned to drugs and fucked up his life.

But I learned toting around all that hate in your heart is a heavy burden. I'm just glad we fixed that shit. Though, I have to say I finally understand where Chase was back then. I've used drugs lately to escape, too. It's an easy fix.

Just like violence, which is what I'm about to do.

However, one thing is different from Chase's past: I won't let my ass end up in prison.

So why am I taking a chance like this?

Because I have to; I'm committed to this shit now. And if this thing goes down how Cass and I planned, we will be rid of Paul…for good.

The plan is a good one, I think. I'm supposed to pick up Cass straight-away after the deed is done. She and I will then head down to Mexico, to lay low for a while.

I figure we can find an empty beach somewhere. We can live in a tent, and I'll find some kind of work for money. Cassie says she'll work, too.

So, yeah, we'll make it. And someday maybe I can return.

I sure hope that's true, because thinking on it now, I know for sure I'm gonna miss my mom...and my brother. They're all I've really got in this shitty world.

My eyes blur with tears, and I swipe them away. "Pussy," I hiss. "Man up, dude."

I turn onto Vulture Mine Road.

Shit. This is far too real.

Glad I skipped the pills Cassie had at her house. I'd really be a wreck if I'd thrown back a few of those. Partying, glad I've slowed that shit down.

Or, rather, I've tried to.

Cassie, though, she's one crazy chick. She's all about getting fucked up. I just haven't been into it much lately. Things in my life have been better, and I haven't felt that need to shut things out.

Glancing up at my reflection in the rearview mirror, I ask, "So, why are you doing this shit now, dumbass?"

I don't have an answer—not one for myself, not one for the world—so I focus back on the road. I'm waylaid, though, when my eyes are drawn to the glint of something silver lying on the passenger seat.

The gun.

I glance over at the pistol I bought from Chase's ex-dealer, Kyle Tanner.

That dude, what a trip.

Snorting, I reach over and grab the gun. I rest the piece in my lap, but when the cold metal starts to feel like it's seeping through my jeans and right into my fucking skin, I move the gun back to the seat next to me.

I return to focusing on my task at hand as I continue down the road. It will be dark soon, and already there are lights ahead. I shudder when I realize the glow is from Paul's trailer, less than a mile away.

That trailer is the only sign of civilization for miles.

I hit the gas, driving beyond the trailer. Eventually, I pull off and park in a truck turnout.

Shutting down the engine, I whisper to dead air, "Showtime, kid."

Then again, maybe not.

I may sound all confident, but it's a lie, a sham. The truth is I'm scared to death. And that makes me just kind of freeze up on the spot.

Dude, this is real, I tell myself for the hundredth time.

What's it going to feel like to kill someone? Damn, that is some serious jail time if I am caught. Not to mention the moral aspect. Sure, Paul is a prick, but this is fucking murder.

"I am too sober for this shit," I mutter.

I don't want drugs—I need to be sharp—but I sure could use another shot right now. Too bad I didn't think to grab one of the bottles of booze before leaving Cassie's place. I had no idea my buzz would wear off so quickly.

I guess coming to grips with the fact you're about to off someone has a way of sobering you up.

I pick up the gun and check to make sure it's loaded.

I know it is, but it's an opportunity to stall.

Before I open the car door, I think about a conversation I had with Chase a couple of days ago. He asked me about Cass. He wanted to know if I loved her. My reply was, "I guess."

Chase then told me I was too young to be involved in something so serious; especially when my best answer as to whether or not I loved my girlfriend was "I guess."

I was only being truthful with my response. Sure, I tell Cassie I love her—and a part of me does—but that wasn't what Chase was asking.

He wanted to know if Cassie was my Kay.

And that I don't know.

I'd like to hope she is—that'd be cool—but I kind of know deep inside she is not.

"So, why the fuck are you about to murder someone for her then?" I ask myself aloud.

I push the thought away swiftly.

"Let's just get this done," I murmur, opening the car door, at last.

I step out and walk up to the road.

There is not a soul in sight.

The lights in Paul's trailer flicker shades of blue. He must be watching TV, changing the channels. Good, let him be distracted; that way I'll get the jump on him.

Walking along the side of the road, closing in on Paul's trailer, I review the plan. It's simple, really.

Find Paul.

Kill Paul.

Get the fuck out of Dodge.

So if it's so simple, why am I having doubts?

No time to think on it further. I'm at the trailer.

I hurry to the back, where I take a quick peek in a dirt-smeared window.

Paul is inside, of course. He's sitting on a reclining chair, and, as I thought, watching TV. I remind myself that the reason he's even home and in the trailer is because he's expecting Cassie.

Prick. I raise the gun so the muzzle rests against the glass.

I could shoot him from here. The back of his head is facing my way, and I have a good angle.

I close one eye and aim.

And aim.

And aim again.

Shit. My hand is shaking too much. In fact, I'm shaking so much that the gun *tap-tap-taps* at the window before I can steady my arm enough to lower it to my side.

And now I am fucked.

"What the hell was that?" Paul bellows from inside the trailer.

Fear overtakes me. It consumes me. I absolutely cannot do this. I'm out of my league here. I am not a killer. Cass and I will have to find another way to take care of Paul. Killing him is obviously not going to be the answer. I just don't have it in me to commit murder in cold blood.

Sorry, Cassie.

I run to the front of the trailer just as Paul emerges from the door.

I take off—faster, faster—but he catches up to me and tackles me, shoving me to the ground. I'm pinned, but I still struggle and fight.

I get the gun pointed at the prick at one point, but he's in his twenties and I'm only in my teens. He's a man, and I'm a boy.

Paul is much stronger and easily wrestles the .45 from my grasp.

Pointing the gun—*my* gun—in my face, he spits out, "You little fuck, what are you doing out here? And what's with the gun? You and that little bitch come up with this shit? You think you can come here and just shoot me?" He laughs. "Guess that plan is fucked all to hell now, huh?"

He chuckles again, but underneath he sounds outraged.

Somehow I muster the courage to say, "Just stay the hell away from Cass, all right?"

Paul's response is another laugh.

And then he quits laughing and hits me in the side of

the head with the gun. That shit hurts like hell.

"Fuck," I grunt as hot blood begins to trickle down my temple.

Paul palms the gun and smirks down at me. *Evil bastard.* It's clear from the angle of his body that he's about to slam the .45 down on my face. I close my eyes and wince, waiting for the sure to be bone-crushing blow.

But it never comes.

Instead, I open my eyes and watch as someone behind Paul delivers one solid hit to his head. With what, I don't know.

Paul crumples onto me and I am blinded by his bulk. I struggle to escape, pushing at his limp form.

Suddenly, someone pulls Paul off of me.

When I'm free, I look up and find my rescuer — Chase.

"Should I even be surprised?" I say, astounded, shocked, and happy all at the same time.

"You all right?" my big brother asks as he offers me his hand.

I take his hand and let him lift me to my feet. "Yeah, I think so," I reply.

Once I'm upright, I brush myself off, glance over at Paul. He's prone on his back, not moving.

Turning back to Chase, I see a bloody pipe in his hand. "You hit him with that?" I ask, eyes widening.

Chase nods grimly as he tosses the heavy piece of steel to the ground.

Shit, we can't leave things like this.

Swiftly, and with no hesitation, I drop to my knees. With the edge of my T-shirt, I pick up the pipe and wipe away my brother's prints.

"What are you doing?" Chase asks.

"Fuck, man…" I glance up at my brother, who will clearly do anything to save me. "I don't care if you killed him," I state. "But I won't stand by and let you go back to prison."

FOURTEEN

Chase

A MURDER rap...
Great, that's just what I need. With my record, I'll never again see the light of day.

Thankfully, though, when I fall to my knees next to what looks like a lifeless body, I notice Paul's chest is rising and falling.

"Thank God," I breathe out, relieved. "He's still alive."

Will, who is done cleaning my prints from the pipe, comes over and kneels down next to me. "What should we do now?" he asks in a shaky voice.

Pulling out the cell phone from the back pocket of my jeans, I say, "I think we better call an ambulance."

Will grimaces. "That means the police will come."

I rake my hand through my hair. "I know." I exhale resignedly. "But what other choice do we have, Will?"

He shrugs and looks away. I know he feels bad for this idiotic stunt.

"You're not going to get into any trouble, right?" he wants to know. "I mean, you did what you had to do to get him off me. He was about to crush my face."

"All true," I say. "I'm sure the police will understand." *Yeah, right.*

Will may have cleaned up the pipe, but the police will still see Paul was hit by something. And then there's the gun—Will's prints are all over that thing.

I glance at Will...then at the gun lying in the dirt.

"What?" Will asks. "What are you thinking, Chase?"

"Just give me a minute," I reply. "I need to think this through."

He nods. "Okay."

My brother bought the gun illegally, so there's no record of the purchase. Hell, the serial number is probably scratched off. But if the police learn the truth of Will's transaction with Kyle Tanner, my brother will end up in a shitload of trouble.

Not going to happen.

My decision is made.

As I rise to my feet, I take off my T-shirt. Wrapping the dark cotton material around my hand, I reach down and pick up the gun. After wiping the .45 clean of all prints, I place it back on the ground.

But then I reconsider, and move the gun over to Paul's limp grasp.

"Chase," Will says warily. Leaning in to me, he whispers, "Do you really think putting it there is a good idea? Isn't that, like, tampering with evidence or some shit?"

I raise a brow. "So says the kid who just cleaned my prints off a metal pipe."

"Hmm, point taken," Will retorts.

After I put my shirt back on, I make the call to 9-1-1.

Next, I call Kay. She's only a half-mile down the road,

but I can't leave my brother alone with Paul while I go retrieve her. What if the perverted prick wakes up?

Kay answers before the first ring is even completed.

"Chase," she says shakily, her tone sounding frightened and frantic. "Are you okay? Where's Will? Did you find him before he did anything stupid? Do you need any help?"

"Hey, hey, calm down, babe," I reply. "We're both okay."

I hear her breathe out a sigh of relief. "Thank God."

"Will is with me," I continue. "Stay where you are. We'll come to you after we talk to the police."

"The police? Oh, Chase."

"Don't worry," I say. "Everything is okay now."

I proceed to tell Kay an abbreviated story, enough to ease her fears and keep her in the car.

"Okay," she assures me. "I'll wait here."

After I wrap up with Kay, I go to stand next to my brother. His temple is still trickling blood, so I reach over and gently wipe at the cut on his head.

Will winces, and I ask, "Does it hurt?"

He shrugs. "A little."

"It's not too deep, but we'll have the paramedics take a look at it, okay?"

"Okay," Will whispers, eyes downcast.

He's staring down at his sneakered feet, so I nudge his shoulder with mine. "Hey, you want to talk about it?"

"Nothing to say," Will replies flatly. "I made a stupid mistake, Chase. I should've never come out here. I should have just given you the right gun the day you asked for it."

I drape an arm around my brother's defeated shoulders. "Don't worry about that shit now. It's over."

Will breathes in deeply. Slowly, he starts to speak, but then he stops.

Finally, after a few minutes, he says in a low voice, "I don't know if Cassie and I are much good for each other. Early on things were all right, but lately it seems like shit turns so toxic when we're together."

I make a scoffing sound, but hold my tongue.

Truthfully, I'd like to see Will get away from Cassie. The thing that bound them together initially—shared loss—is not enough anymore. Cassie's problems are for adults—like her mom and the police—to handle. Will is only fifteen and dealing with enough shit of his own.

"What do you think you're going to do?" I carefully inquire.

"Break up with her, I guess." His gaze lifts and zones in on me. "Do you think I should?"

I throw my hands up, as if to say *don't ask me*. "Hey, you have to decide that for yourself, bro."

Despite my true feelings, I am not going to lead Will one way or the other. Whatever he decides, the decision must be his. Anything else, like my interference, will only breed resentment. I know this from experience.

"I'll think about it," Will says at last. And then he abruptly adds, "Did you know Mom wants me to go talk to someone? Like a counselor or some shit."

"How do you feel about that?" I softly inquire. "Do you think it will help?"

Will shrugs, and just like that he's back to staring at the ground. "I don't know, Chase," he says. "I really don't know. Maybe…possibly."

I want to talk more with Will about the counseling, but sirens in the background put an end to that discussion… for now. Not to mention there's something Will and I need to get straight—our story about what happened here tonight.

"Hey," I say to Will. "We need to have our stories straight before the cops get here. What are you planning on saying?"

"Mostly the truth, I guess. Nothing about the gun, though. We can pretend it was his all along, right?"

I glance at the .45 resting in Paul's outstretched hand. "Right," I say.

We continue to go over our stories so they corroborate perfectly.

I clear my throat when we're done, and Will says, "I'll probably get in trouble for driving Cass's car without a license."

"Yeah," I agree, "most likely."

I don't add what I'm sure we are both thinking: *It's better than being in trouble for having an illegal firearm in your possession. One you fully intended on using.*

When the police and paramedics do arrive, Will and I stick to our agreed-upon stories, with Will explaining to the police that he came out here merely to talk with Paul. And only because he was tired of Paul's continued harassment of Cassie.

"I thought maybe I could reason with him man-to-man," Will explains to the officer taking our stories down.

The policeman nods and turns to me. "And you, how did you end up here?"

"Uh..." I clear my throat. "I came out after Will's girlfriend told me he wanted to talk with Paul. I had a feeling things might get heated, and I wanted to be here to protect my little brother."

The cop glances at the pipe on the ground. "You didn't hit him with that, did you?"

"No," I reply. "I only used my hands."

I don't think the cop really buys it, but he doesn't press. And little wonder. Turns out, there are multiple APBs out on Paul. Not just the one for violating the restraining order to stay away from Cassie, but for other things too, similar things to what he was doing to Will's girlfriend.

My brother and I are informed that Paul has an outstanding arrest warrant out on him in another state. We are told he used to live in some tiny town in Arizona, where he's suspected of soliciting under-age girls online for sex.

"Sick fuck," I murmur when the cop is finished with *that* particular story.

"He's going to be going away for a long, long time," the officer states. Turning to Will, he adds, "You and your girlfriend will never have to worry about this man ever bothering you again."

"Good," Will says.

With our statements on record, Will and I are free to leave. The police make arrangements for Cassie's car to be towed back to her house.

Together, Will and I walk away from Paul's trailer and head toward the rental car down the road.

"You lucked out," I say to Will.

The officers at the scene chose not to write him up for driving without a license.

"Just don't do it again," one burly cop admonished.

"No, sir," Will replied.

Now, on the way to the car, Will says, "You're not kidding. I was one lucky guy tonight."

"You sure were," I agree, "in a lot of ways."

Will doesn't disagree. In fact, he thanks me for saving his ass.

"That's what big brothers are for." I reach over and ruffle his hair, carefully, though, so as to avoid the cut on his temple. The paramedics bandaged it before we left, but I'm sure it still hurts like hell.

Will half-heartedly attempts to push me away. "Stop it," he complains.

Since it's been a rough night, I leave him be.

A couple of minutes later, right before we reach the

car, Will slows to a stop.

I stop next to him and ask, "What's up?"

"Uh..." he trails off.

I jerk my head, indicating the rental car where Kay is waiting. "When she notices us, she's going to be out of that car in a heartbeat. You better tell me now if you have something to say."

Exhaling, Will says, "Since this is all over, I was wondering if you and Kay plan on heading back to Ohio soon."

"Pretty soon, yeah. School starts in a week and a half, and Kay needs to be back before then."

"That's right," Will says. "She teaches first grade in the school we painted the mural in, right?"

I nod as I think about those summer days that seem so long ago.

"Hey, Chase." Will's eyes meet mine. "Is there any way you, just you, could stay a little while longer?"

I shake my head, and Will swiftly adds, "Even just one more week would be good."

"I don't know, Will." I rake my fingers through my hair, uncertain. Even though I'm sure Kay would be fine with me staying under most circumstances, I don't think spending our first few weeks as a married couple apart is going to go over all that well.

But Will sends me such a pleading look that I can't refuse.

"One more week," I say, relenting. "Not a single day longer, though."

My brother's face now positively beams. "Thank you, Chase," he says. "And I'll tell Kay myself that I promise I won't keep you two apart a minute beyond one extra week."

Just then, in the distance, a jagged streak of lightning brightens the sky, giving me the most morbid sense of foreboding.

FIFTEEN

Kay

I DISCOVER plans have changed when Chase and I are back at the house.

"So…" I say. "We're not going to drive back to Ohio on the motorcycle?"

I try not to sound dejected, but I can't hide my dismay as Chase and I walk up to our bedroom.

"Baby girl…" Chase stops at the top of the stairs and wraps his arms around me. "I am so sorry. It looks like we'll have to fly back."

"Yeah, separately," I say, sighing.

'Yes, separately, but I'll be back in Ohio not much longer after you."

"One week later," I reply, frowning. "Yes, I know."

Chase doesn't need an upset me to deal with, so I try to smile.

I feel so torn, though. I can't ask Chase not to stay with his brother. Will needs him. Only problem is, I need Chase too. I'll never say this to him, however. I refuse to make him choose, because, ultimately, I know Chase Gartner will always choose me.

That knowledge gives me the peace to stay silent…and to remain silent the next night when Chase and I are lying in bed, the specter of our impending separation weighing on us both.

"What are you thinking?" he asks as I stare up at the ceiling.

I turn and nuzzle into his strong chest. "Oh, nothing, really," I reply.

"So you're sure you're okay with me staying in Vegas this next week?" he asks. It's a question that has been asked and answered too many times to count.

Still, I reassure him, "Yes, absolutely, Chase. I'll be so busy during the first few days of school that I probably won't even notice you're not around."

That remark gets his attention.

Raising his head from the pillow and peering down at me, he says, "Yeah, right."

"Okay," I acquiesce, smiling. "Maybe that's an exaggeration."

"Even if that's true"—Chase rolls on top of me—"I better make sure you have lots of hot memories to keep you going."

Wrapping my legs around his strong body, I say, "Hmm, hot memories, huh? Sounds like a plan."

And then we get started on making what turns out to be a *very hot* memory.

The following morning Abby leaves with Will for their first family counseling session. The house is quiet, since Greg's still away on business. Chase and I are only too happy to take advantage of all the alone time by spending the morning in bed.

"So, what do you want to do today?" Chase asks as he slides me off of him. He props himself up on one elbow, facing me.

It's been a morning full of loving, lots of loving, but it's time to cool things down.

"Hmm," I say. "Let's go see something interesting."

"Interesting?" he says. "Like what?"

"Like a major tourist attraction or something."

"Okay," Chase replies. He ponders for a minute then says, "How about a trip down to the Grand Canyon?"

I've never been there, and I'm quick to reply, "Ooh, I like that idea."

"But before we go..." Chase raises a suggestive brow.

Reaching over, he skims his hand down to the curve of my hip, where he squeezes and pulls me to him.

"What?" I ask, playing clueless.

"Oh, you know what," he says.

And then the talking ends.

So much for cooling things down. Let's just say it takes us an extra hour before we are out the door and on the road.

When we eventually make it down to Arizona—late in the day—I am awed by the Grand Canyon.

Standing at a South Rim observation point, with the just-beginning-to-set sun sizzling into the horizon, I marvel, "Wow, Chase. This is just... I have no words. Just wow."

Chase comes up from behind me and encircles me in his arms. "It is amazing, isn't it?" he murmurs in my ear.

"Now I wish we'd gotten here sooner," I confess. "I don't think I want to turn around and leave."

"We don't have to go." Chase nuzzles his chin in my hair. "We can stay overnight if you want."

"Really?" I lean back against his hard chest. "What

would we do? Sleep in the car?"

He chuckles, his chest rumbling against my back. "No, no sleeping in the car. I had a feeling you'd like it down here, so I brought along some camping gear. It's in the trunk."

"Ah..." I turn in his arms to face him. "That's why you wanted to take the rental car and not the bike."

"You found me out," he says, laughing. And then, in a more serious tone, "I wanted to surprise you with the option of staying."

I reach up and touch the side of his face. "You always think of everything, don't you?"

"I just want to make you happy, Kay," he replies.

"I am happy," I assure him. "I'm very happy."

And it's true. In this moment, I couldn't be any happier.

For whatever reason, the canyon is not particularly busy, so Chase and I retrieve our gear from the trunk, secure a camping permit from the park office in no time, and proceed to hike down to the canyon base by nightfall.

We find a good spot to set up our tent and unroll the two sleeping bags Chase had the foresight to bring. After we're completely settled, Chase makes a small fire. And then we sit in front of Chase's fire, shoulder-to-shoulder, a blanket wrapped around our backs as we share a canteen of water and a couple of energy bars.

"Look at all the stars," I muse as I gesture to the velvety black sky where a billion dots of light twinkle and glow.

Chase shrugs the blanket off our shoulders and stretches it wide behind us on the desert floor.

As he leans us back gently, he says, "Ah, now there's a better view."

I snuggle into him and place my head on his chest. "I swear I've never seen so many stars," I murmur.

He kisses the top of my head, and asks, "Would you say there are more stars here than back in Harmony Creek?"

The reminder of our rooftop picnic makes me smile.

"There may be more here," I reply, "but our stars back home will always be the best."

Chase chuckles. "Hate to break it to you, sweet girl, but these are the same exact stars."

"Ah, don't ruin it for me," I tease.

Feeling playful, I roll to my stomach and place a hand on his chest. "And too bad for you, if you do ruin it," I add cryptically.

With his hand going to mine—covering, holding—he inquires, "What does that mean, babe?"

"Oh, I don't know," I coyly respond.

"Tell me," he insists.

"Okay," I relent. "I was thinking if these stars are different, then we should make love under them. Kind of christen them out here in the desert, you know?" I shrug. "But, hey, since they're the same, why bother—"

I get no further. Chase swiftly flips me to my back and pins me under his solid body.

With his lips grazing mine, he whispers, "I was wrong. Oh, so wrong. These stars are most definitely different"—he kisses me fully on the mouth—"and most definitely in need of christening."

"Well," I murmur, breathless. "When you put it like that…"

Chase and I then make love under the stars—once, twice, numerous times throughout the night. It feels as nature intended—bodies bare and joined, as man and woman, as husband and wife.

I love Chase with my body, yes, but also with my heart and soul. And he loves me in return, in the same ways, as indicated by his tender kisses and reverent touches as we move as one.

When I think I have nothing left—*no baby, no more,* I cry out—he shows me how wrong I am.

With measured thrusts, he urges, "Come for me one more time, Kay."

I lift my hips, my body knowing better than I, even as I utter, "I can't."

"You can," he rasps, his pace increasing.

And with Chase in me, on me, over me, and around me, I discover he is right.

One final time, in the deep of the night and under the stars, I come undone for my husband, Chase Gartner.

SIXTEEN

Chase

S ENDING Kay back to Harmony Creek without me
turns out to be one of the hardest things I've ever
had to do. She's become such a part of my life, and
our bond transcends the marriage vows we took.

Put in the simplest terms, when Kay breathes, I breathe.

Before my love boards the plane, she wraps her little
arms around me best as she can. In a choked-up voice, she
says, "Do you realize this will be the first time we've been
apart since we first met?"

Surely that can't be right.

"Wait," I say. "We spent our nights apart in the early
days. Remember, we didn't sleep in the same bed until
after we were together for almost a month."

The first night we ever spent together was when Kay
showed up on my doorstep, frightened and hurt from
the junkie who had accosted her in her then-apartment
parking lot.

With her cheek pressed firmly to my chest, she murmurs, "Still, Chase, we were together every day...even when I was mad at you over the incident with Missy."

She trails off, and I murmur, "Ah, yes, the incident with Missy."

Kay was pissed when she learned of an encounter I had, of the sexual variety, with her friend. Although, in my defense, the encounter happened before I met Kay. And she wasn't so much mad over the event, she was pissed I'd never told her.

But that was then, and this is now.

Peering up at me, Kay says, "Even then, Chase, even when I was angry, I was always right next door to you. I never left your side."

"No, you didn't," I reply.

Recalling the night we reconciled, I smile down at her. "You were right there with me. I saw the lights in your apartment. And when you came outside, you forgave me. I was playing old records, and we danced under the stars, remember?"

"Of course I remember," she says, her cheek returning to rest against my chest. "That was also the night I told you about Sarah."

Pressing my lips to the top of her head, I murmur, "You trusted me enough to share that horrible night with me."

"And you trusted me enough to forgive me," she whispers.

"There was nothing to forgive, Kay. You did nothing wrong the night Sarah passed away. You were a victim as much as she was."

She looks up at me slowly. Her eyes hold mine, bleeding truth and caramel. "Still, Chase, you gave me the absolution I sought."

"Baby..."

My heart aches with the sadness she still carries. Her

pain is my pain. These burdens of ours, we share.

I hold her tightly. "Do you want me to go back with you to Ohio today? Because, I will, Kay, I will."

My brother needs me, yes, but I will board that plane in a heartbeat if my wife needs me more.

But she shakes her head and assures me, "No. I want you to stay here for Will. I'll be fine, Chase. Like I told you, school will keep me busy. And I'll be waiting for you when you come home to Harmony Creek."

"It's not Harmony Creek that's my home," I tell her. "It's you, Kay. *You* are my home."

"Come back to me soon, then."

Kay is practically sobbing and has to pull away to get herself together.

When the plane starts to board, I reach out and wipe away the last of her tears. "Be strong," I urge her.

She taps my chest. "You, too."

And then she is gone.

I am left alone, and, fuck, do I ever *feel* alone.

"How am I going to make it through this next week," I mumble to myself as I turn to leave the terminal.

I have no choice, though, but to be fine. I have to be strong for Will.

I smile. That kid is sure to keep me occupied, too. I know I can count on that.

School for Kay kicks off next Tuesday, the day after Labor Day, but Will doesn't start tenth grade for another week. We're sure to have plenty of time to hang out and bond.

And over the next couple of days, that is exactly how things go. Will and I spend all our time together.

Then, on Sunday afternoon, Will asks me if I can do something for him.

"Hey, Chase," he says, walking into the kitchen at lunchtime. "Can you do me a favor?"

I am at the table, finishing up a sandwich, and between bites, I ask, "Sure. What's up?"

Will plops down in a chair across from me. His greens turn somber as he asks, "Can you take me over to Cassie's house this afternoon?"

Arching an eyebrow, I say, "I thought you two broke up the other day."

Will frowns and runs his fingers through his messy hair. "No, I couldn't do it then. That's why I need you to drive me over there today."

I push away my plate. "Sure, I can take you."

Sighing, Will adds, "I figure a face-to-face is better than a text or a call. Cassie at least deserves that, right?"

"You know best," I say, unsure of how to proceed.

Ending relationships is uncharted territory for me. Before Kay, I didn't bother with girlfriends. I had lots of women, sure, but nothing ever lasted longer than what it took to get off, get her off, and get out.

"Can we leave soon?" Will asks, a little desperately. "I want to get this over with."

"Yeah, no problem." I give him a pat on the shoulder as I stand. When I take my plate over to the sink to wash it off, I throw out over my shoulder, "I'll grab my keys in a sec and meet you out by the car."

"Thanks, bro," Will replies before he leaves.

With Will out of the room, under my breath, I murmur, "Shit. I hope this goes well."

A half an hour later, we are sitting in the rental car, idling in Cassie's driveway.

I turn to Will and ask, "Want me to take off for a while? I can come back for you in a couple of hours."

"No." Will shakes his head, his expression grim. "Can you just wait here? I won't be too long."

When he glances over at me, I give him what I hope is an encouraging smile. "Yeah, sure, Will. I'll wait here. But no rush, Take as long as you need."

Once Will is in the house, I hunker down in the driver's seat, prepared to wait it out for the long haul.

Who knows how long this could take, I think.

Imagine my surprise when Will returns only ten minutes later.

"Hell, that didn't take long," I remark as he jumps into the front seat and tugs on the seatbelt.

"Can we just go," he rasps, his head turned away.

"Are you okay?"

Digging the heel of his hand into his eyes, Will says in a muffled voice, "No, I'm not okay, Chase. But please, please, just drive. I need to get out of here."

"No problem, bro."

I reverse out of the driveway, but before we can make a clean getaway, I catch a glimpse of a crying Cassie in the window. She's partway hidden by the long curtains, but I see her. She's crying and watching, watching Will leave her house, watching my brother leave her life.

"Hey, I know this is hard," I say softly. "But let's go home and—"

"I don't want to go home," Will snaps, cutting me off. "Can we just go somewhere other than home? Anywhere but there is good. Please, Chase."

"Is there somewhere you think you'd want to go?" I ask.

"Yes." Will looks over at me with watery and soulful eyes. "Can you take me to where Dad is buried?"

His request floors me, and I can't find any words to reply for a few seconds. When I get a grip on the emotions his request has dredged up, I ask, "Have you ever been to Dad's grave?"

"Yeah." He blows out a breath. "But it was a long time ago."

"Did Cassie drive you there?"

I am curious as to who took Will to Dad's grave.

"No," he replies. "I went there with Mom."

Whoa.

"Mom went to Dad's grave?"

I am stunned by this admission, but Will confirms, "Yeah. Sometimes she'd be feeling all nostalgic and shit. That's when she'd ask me to go to the cemetery with her."

"Huh," I utter, while thinking, *Wow, Mom is full of surprises…even now.*

But I don't have time to lose myself in trying to figure out my mom. I promptly take my brother to where he wants to go—our father's grave.

"When was the last time you were here?" Will asks once we're standing side-by-side at Jack Gartner's final resting place.

The stone angel is casting us in her long shadow, as if she's watching over all three Gartner men—two for just a little while, and one for infinity.

"I was out here a couple of weeks ago," I reply to Will, my eyes flicking from the angel to my brother.

"Seriously?" he says, sounding surprised. "Did you come out here all by yourself?"

"No. I was with Kay."

Will opens his mouth, but then pauses, until at last, he says, "You really love Kay, don't you?"

"More than anything, bro."

"Wow," he says with no irony. "I sure hope I find something like that someday."

I put my arm around him, and he leans into me. "You will," I assure him, "you will."

I'm hopeful my brother will someday find a love like the one I have with my wife. He deserves that much in life.

We spend the next hour—or maybe it's two—at our father's gravesite. My brother and I don't say a hell of a lot when we first sit down next to the stone marker, the sandy earth cool in the shadow of the angel.

But eventually Will starts opening up.

"My therapist thought it'd be a good idea for me to come out here."

"Oh, yeah?" I reply, pulling my knees up to my chest. "Is that so?"

"Yeah." Will mirrors my posture, and with his chin resting on one knee, he says, "She wanted Mom to bring me out, but" — his eyes slide meaningfully over to me — "I'm glad you're the one with me here instead."

I want Will to keep talking; it's not just his therapist who thinks this is good for him.

So I carefully reply, "I'm glad I'm here with you, too."

"I don't know how I feel about Dad," Will continues after a beat. "I mean, I still love him, Chase. Like, a lot. Is that crazy or what?"

"It's not crazy at all, Will."

"Do you still love him?"

I rub the palm of my hand across my forehead, where sweat is beading. "Yeah, bro, of course I still love him."

"You were mad at him, though," Will says in a tone that is far from accusing, just matter-of-fact. "For a long time, you were really pissed at Dad."

"I was," is my simple response.

I haven't completely made peace with my dead father, but I'm closer to it than ever before. Still, how do you put feelings like that into words?

I don't have to, I soon discover. It is Will who needs to talk.

And talk he does.

"I was angry like you, Chase," he says, "For a long time, too."

"What about now?" I ask.

He shrugs. "I don't know. I feel bad that Dad gave up on us so easily. And I sure as hell don't want to end up like him. That desperate, you know?"

I nod. "I hear what you're saying."

After a long pause, he says, "I guess, mostly, nowadays, I just feel kind of sad about it all. Sad and disappointed that it went down the way it did."

He's not kidding.

Sighing, I agree. "I know, Will. I feel pretty much the same way as you."

We sit and soak on that for a while, and then, out of the blue, and rather fervently, Will proclaims, "I won't let you down, Chase, I won't. I'm not Dad. No more bullshit from me, I promise. I am always going to be here for you, *always*."

Shit, my kid brother is making the promises I should be making to him.

"Hey, don't worry about me." I drape an arm around him. "I love you, Will, no matter what. It's not *your* responsibility to make up for what we're missing thanks to Dad taking his own life."

"It's not yours, either," Will says. "Still, isn't that exactly what you've been trying to do?" — Will knows me far too well — "You've been trying to fill the void Dad left for years."

I laugh. Not a happy laugh, just one of acceptance and resignation.

"Yeah," I concede, "I guess you're right. Maybe I was always trying to fill the void left by Dad. I guess I still am."

"No maybes or guesses about it, dude." Will nudges me, smiling.

"I don't know if that will ever change," I admit.

"Not with me, either," Will states.

"Guess it's not such a bad thing, eh?" I nudge Will. "This watching out for each other thing."

Smiling, he replies, "Not a bad thing at all, big brother."

In the hot Nevada desert, shaded by a stone angel that

impacted me so much I had her likeness inked on my back, I come to the realization that Jack Gartner may be dead, yes, but he lives on in Will and me. And while we will always feel the loss of our dad, we have each other to pick up the slack.

Maybe what I've been searching for all this time has been here right in front of me all along.

In that moment, because of my brother, because of where we are today and how far we've come, I find true peace with my dad.

SEVENTEEN

Kay

HOME—HARMONY Creek. It's not home, though, without Chase.

He told me at the airport in Vegas that I am his home. Well, he is my home, too. That fact is never clearer than when everywhere I turn, and everywhere I go, I am faced with reminders of the man I love, the man I now call my husband.

At the farmhouse, Chase is there. He invades my every thought.

When I return home from work and stand on the porch, I hesitate before opening the door. I picture Chase behind the screen door, as he was one late June night when I needed him, when he was there for me. His blue eyes were filled with so much sadness for me that night… and so much anger for the man who assaulted me.

Inside the house, Chase's presence is there, too.

I see him in the bathroom, standing in front of me as I

sat perched on the counter. He's holding ice to my cheek, and he is kissing me. Again, it's the same fateful night I ended up at his door. As he fitted his body to mine, I wanted him–oh, how I had yearned.

But Chase made me wait.

And the waiting was so worth it.

Downstairs, there's little reprieve from my onslaught of memories. Chase is in the kitchen, he's in the living room. He's in the dining room, sketching at the table.

But I miss his presence most in the room where we share a bed.

I smell Chase in the sheets; I feel his warmth. And when I roll to my back and peer up at the wall behind the bed, I am met with the Eiffel Tower oil pastel Chase drew for me. The sketch shines with my man's heart and soul.

Late one night, waking from a fitful sleep, I feel empty and alone. I reach for Chase.

But he, of course, is not there.

I seek solace at Holy Trinity, both the church and the school, and I find some relief. On the first day of school, I am kept busy, so there's no time to dwell on Chase. A fresh set of bright-eyed, eager first-graders require my attention and keep thoughts of my missing love at bay.

But when I'm not busy with the kids, I realize, Chase, like how it is at home, is all around the school. His work is everywhere—in the bright walls he painted this summer, in the newly replaced lighting, even in my own classroom I can't get away from the onslaught of memories.

I stare at the bright red ceramic apple on my desk, remembering how Chase picked it up the day I took him on a tour of the school. He couldn't quit fiddling with things—like the apple—that day. I found him to be very "hands-on," and, consequently, I couldn't wait for his hands to end up on me.

And they did. Oh, how they did.

Chase's hands have left invisible marks; his skin is seared to mine. I'm branded by him, by his love, by his intensity.

At the end of the day, as I'm leaving the school, I am again reminded of Chase.

On the wall across from the front doors, the mural he and Will painted in July glows in full glory, bathed in the slant of the late-day sun.

Out in the parking lot, I'm still thinking of Chase. So much so that when someone calls my name, it takes me a minute to respond.

I'm almost at my car, and when I stop and turn around, I discover it is Missy Metzger who is trying to get my attention.

Taking a step in her direction as she hurries over to me, I wave. "Hey, Missy."

She waves back. "Kay, wait up a sec. I want to talk to you."

"Okay, sure."

Before she reaches me, I note that Missy looks good. She appears to be fully recovered from the car accident and the subsequent miscarriage she suffered. When I left Harmony Creek a few weeks ago, Missy was in a bad depression. She didn't want to see me or anyone, really. But today, dressed in a dark floral dress with her ashy-blonde hair flowing down her back in bouncy curls, she looks great.

I smile when she reaches me. "Hey, girl, how've you been?" I touch her arm.

"I've been good." She places her hand on her chest to catch her breath. "Oh, my goodness, I'm so out of shape. Anyway, I didn't want to miss you. It feels like forever since we talked."

"It has been a while." I agree.

"Too long," she says.

There's a moment where our eyes meet. We both seem to be pondering whether to bring up the accident, but the point becomes moot when Missy instead says, "So...how was Las Vegas?"

"It was good." I lean against the side of my car, preparing to spend some time catching up. Truthfully, I'm happy to see Missy, and I'm relieved she's all right.

Glancing around, brow creasing, Missy asks, "Hey, where is Chase? Is he not working today?"

"Uh, actually..." I clear my throat. "He's not here. He decided to stay an extra week out west."

Missy shoots me a look of concern. "Is everything okay, Kay?"

"Yes, yes, everything is fine." I wave my hand in the air dismissively. "Will just wanted a little extra time with his brother, that's all. And, well, I knew I'd be busy here with the first week of school."

Missy nods and replies, "Oh, that's good," but I can tell that her hearing Will's name is a reminder of his friend, Jared.

Jared was the one who ran into Missy's car, with his parent-funded Jaguar. Sadly, Missy's cheap little car was no match. Jared walked away unharmed, but Missy... well, she didn't fare so well.

Quietly, I ask her how she's been, like how she's *really* been.

"I really am okay, Kay," she insists. "I've accepted what happened if that's what you're wondering."

"That's good, I guess," I quietly reply.

"It is," she says. "But Kay, can I tell you something?"

"Yes, absolutely."

"I haven't had to go through all of this alone. Someone, someone you'd never expect, has been a great help."

Curious, I raise a brow. "Oh? Who's been helping you?"

Missy smiles surreptitiously. Whoever it is, he or she is

making her happy.

"Believe it or not," she says, at last, "Nick has come back into my life. He's really been there for me, and it's made a world of difference."

Well, he was the father, I think.

"That's great Nick has been there for you," I say, truly happy for Missy. "He's a good guy."

"He really is," Missy agrees. She presses her lips together, suppressing a genuine smile, but she can't help herself. Beaming, she tells me, "Actually, Nick and I are kind of dating now."

"Seriously?" She nods, and I add, "That's wonderful, Missy."

"I know it's kind of a backward way to start things," she says. "But I guess it is what it is."

"Hey, there's no right or wrong way to begin a relationship. I met Chase when we literally ran into each other in this very parking lot." I wave my hand around to where we're standing. "When all is said and done, what matters is where you and Nick end up."

"Thanks, Kay," she softly responds. "I knew you'd understand."

Yeah, Missy Metzger and I have come a long way. And I'm glad. So glad, in fact, that I long to share with her my happy news—the fact that Chase and I got hitched in Vegas. But our nuptials are still our secret. Chase and I have yet to tell a soul.

So, I decide to wait…for now. I also decide something else as we are standing in the church parking lot— I decide when the time is right, I will ask Missy to be my maid of honor when Chase and I do have our church wedding.

Missy and I talk for a few more minutes, about school, about church things. And then, when we run out of words, we say good-bye, and I then hop in my car and head home.

Back at the house, I can't wait to hear from Chase.

We've talked and texted a bunch the past few days, but I haven't heard much from him today. That thankfully changes when my cell rings and his comforting voice is the first thing I hear when I answer.

There's a smile in my voice as I reply, "Hey, Chase."

"Hey, babe."

I sigh, as does he, and then I tell him. "Damn, I am missing you so much. I swear there are reminders of you everywhere."

He chuckles then says, "I miss you too, Kay. More than you can imagine."

"It's just so good to hear your voice," I say.

And then we talk for a long while. But when it's time to disconnect, I just can't. The ache of missing him has actually begun to hurt.

"Only three more days apart," I whisper, pained. "Do you think we can survive seventy-two more hours?"

"Fuck, I hope so," Chase replies, sighing. "I swear this week apart has felt like a goddamn month."

"For sure," I agree, and in a low voice, I add, "You know what the hardest part has been, though?"

"What's that, sweet girl?"

"Not touching you, Chase. And you, not being here to touch me." I choke back a sob. "It's killing me, I swear."

"Baby, baby," he says, trying to soothe me. "I promise I'll touch you so much when I return home that you'll grow sick of me. You'll be pushing me away."

"Never," I declare. "I could never push you away, Chase."

He laughs. "Wonder if you'll be saying those words twenty years from now."

"Are you kidding?" I scoff. "Trust me, I will."

And then, after a long beat, Chase says, "Kay, I love you so much, baby."

"I love you, too."

"I wouldn't be able to do any of this without you," he whispers. "Helping Will and being strong for him. I know I've stumbled and faltered, but I feel stronger now than I ever have before. Just knowing we're in this together, forever. Marrying you was the best decision, ever."

"Chase…" My heart skips a beat. "Be safe, come back to me soon."

"Three days," he says.

"Three days," I echo.

"We'll make it."

"We sure will."

EIGHTEEN

Chase

FRIDAY finally arrives and it's time to go home. I'm both relieved and excited to head back to Ohio. Mostly, I can't wait to see Kay, but unfortunately, it is only morning, and my flight doesn't leave until three in the afternoon.

More waiting, *fuck*.

Will looks more than a little sulky that I'm leaving Las Vegas. There's some time before I need to head to the airport, so I suggest we grab an early lunch.

That brightens little bro considerably, and he excitedly informs me that he knows of a great little Mexican restaurant in a strip mall not far from the house.

"It's so good, Chase. You'll love it," he enthusiastically states.

He's already heading to the door as I'm grabbing the car keys, and saying, "Cool. Let's go."

Fifteen minutes later, we are at the restaurant in the

strip mall. Will was right, too—the food is pretty damn good.

Over a mound of chips and a bowl of fiery salsa, just how Will and I like it, my brother suddenly blurts out a from-the-heart sounding, "Thank you, Chase. Thank you for everything."

Whoa, serious-talk from Will.

I choose my words carefully for my response as I dip a chip into the hottest salsa I've ever tasted. Before raising my gloppy mess to my mouth, I say, "What exactly do you mean by 'everything'?"

I want Will to elaborate; it's good for him.

"For staying," he says. "And for being here for me like you've been all week. Before then, even. But the past few days have been especially great, like old times."

I know it's hard for my brother to open up like this, but he's doing a commendable job.

Smiling, I tell him, "I'll always be here for you, Will, no matter what."

It's true. I won't ever be my father—I won't leave Will.

His green eyes, eyes that have been nothing but clear lately as he, too, finds the peace to move on, meet mine. "I know that, Chase," he says. "I trust you."

Those three words, spoken by my baby bro, mean the world to me.

"We've come a long way, haven't we, kid?"

Will knows what I mean. I'm referring to our rift and the bumps we encountered while reuniting and rebuilding this fractured relationship.

"Yeah," Will says, smiling, "we sure have come a long way."

After a minute of reflection, on both our parts, I carefully inquire, "Therapy going okay?"

"Yeah, Chase." Will nods once. "It's going real good."

Since Will is being so talkative, I continue with another question. "How are you holding up with Cassie out of your life?"

Will winces, and I'm concerned I've pushed too far. "Sorry," I mumble.

Will shakes his head, and insists, "No, it's okay to ask."

I shrug, as he sighs and rakes a hand through his hair.

"I still miss her, Chase," he says. "But breaking up was the right thing to do...for both of us."

I can't disagree, but I don't want to make a production, so I stick with an affirming nod.

I'm glad there's such an easy camaraderie nowadays when Will and I talk like this. It really does feel like old times. Truthfully, I haven't felt this close to my brother in years. And that makes me want to share something with him, something that is as important to me as all the things he's been sharing are to him.

I clear my throat, and Will looks up. "Everything okay?" he asks.

"Everything is great," I assure him. "It's just..." I search for the right words. "I want to tell you something, Will, but you can't tell Mom. Not yet, anyway."

"Oh, a secret, that's cool." Will laughs, and then he says, "Don't worry, I won't tell Mom a thing."

My eyes meet his, and I just lay it out there. "Kay and I are married."

There's a salsa-laden chip halfway to Will's mouth, and it drops to the table, making a mess.

"Shit..." Will starts to wipe away the spilled salsa with a napkin. "No way, dude. When did this happen? And *where* did this happen? Damn, bro, how do I not know this?"

"One question at a time," I say, laughing. "We got married here in Vegas, like, a couple of weeks ago. We just went to one of the chapels and that was that."

"Wow." Will levels me with a grim expression. "You do realize Mom is going to flip when she finds out."

"Ha," I laugh. "I know she'll be pissed as hell. She's bound to give me shit for years over this stunt."

"No doubt," Will agrees, and then he adds, "I don't envy you, Chase."

"She'll get over it," I say. "And having done things the way Kay and I did is still worth her wrath."

It's true. No amount of grief my mother can give me will ever make me regret the decision to run off and marry the love of my life. You never know what might happen day to day. You can't wait around for everything to be just right.

Will leans back in the booth and blows out a breath. "So, how did all this happen, like, specifically?"

I grab a chip and dip it in the hot salsa. "We just decided to do it one night. We snuck off, drove down to one of those fancy casinos with the nice chapels, and got it done."

"Hey," Will says. "I think this is pretty damn cool. If any two people in this world should be married, it's you and Kay."

I can see he's genuinely happy for me, and I reply with a heartfelt, "Thanks, Will."

He digs back into the chips I've been devouring, and after a minute of crunching, says, "Hell, you gotta get back to Ohio now. You're a newlywed, dude. That's some awesome shit."

"Yeah," I agree, laughing. "It sure is."

Will continues, "Hell, Chase, I'm sure there are things you could be doing in Harmony Creek with Kay right now that are far more fun than hanging out with me." Will waggles his eyebrows, like I don't know what he means, and I shake my head and laugh.

Our entrees arrive, and we dig in like we haven't eaten

in days, putting an end to our convo for the time being.

When we're almost finished with our meals, Will says slowly, "So, I was thinking…"

He trails off, and I prompt, "Yeah? What were you thinking?"

"Well…" He takes a deep breath. "I was wondering if it'd be okay if I fly out to Ohio to visit over Christmas break."

"Shit." I look over at my brother and smile. "I think that sounds like a great idea."

In the past, we've talked about Will visiting this coming winter. But for him to bring it up on his own means he really wants to do it.

We've finally reached a good place, a very good place.

The waitress arrives to clear the table then takes off after a minute, leaving the check. I pull out some money to pay.

"That was a good lunch," I say as I toss some bills on the table.

"It was really good," Will replies. "And the talk we had was even better."

I look over at him and nod sincerely. "For sure."

Out in the parking lot, after Will and I are buckled up in the rental car, I nod to the clock in the dash. "It's almost one. I better drop you off and get my ass to the airport."

"Guess so, Mr. Newlywed," Will says, his voice full of mirth.

I call him a dick, but it's all in good fun. In fact, both of us are laughing as I head to the shopping plaza exit.

The light at the intersection is green, so I hit the gas.

Something feels off, though. And a second later, I detect movement to my left.

Fuck. It's too late to change what is about to happen.

In what feels like slow-motion, Will looks over and yells, "Chase, watch out!"

And at that exact second a car smashes into my side of the car.

The airbag deploys, and I'm jerked to the left, where my head slams into the side window.

And that is the exact point where everything fades to black.

NINETEEN

Will

C HASE cannot be hurt like this. No way. My brother is too strong, too tough, for things to end in this way. But end, it may.

With the weight of that possibility laying heavy on my shoulders, I cry out, "No, no, no." Staring over from the passenger seat, I can't take my eyes off my brother.

I've never seen Chase so still, so un-full of life. He's slumped over the steering wheel, with the deployed air bag lying crumpled and lifeless beneath his barely moving chest.

"At least he's alive," I mutter.

But how much longer does he have? How seriously is he hurt?

I know I need to check, but I can't move. Not at first. I guess I'm in a state of shock or something. So, for another full minute, I continue to stare at my injured and unconscious brother.

Chase is facing in my direction and he looks kind of peaceful. His eyes are closed, no pale blues staring back at me like they should be.

And that is fucked up.

Finally, I get it together and spring into action. Pushing my own deployed air bag out of the way, I reach for Chase, just as a trickle of bright red blood trails down from his forehead.

"Chase." My voice sounds scratchy and rough, and when I'm tugged back by the seatbelt that probably saved my life, I let out a litany of curse words that would probably shock even my brother. That is, if he were conscious.

I'm thankful my life was spared by the seatbelt, but nothing is going to keep me from my brother. Needless to say, I unsnap that motherfucking piece of material and fling it out of the way.

Finally free, I lean over and touch Chase. My first action is to wipe away the blood from his forehead.

But more begins to flow. Like a faucet that's been turned on, blood, bright and red, keeps coming and coming.

"What the fuck," I grind out, my heart racing, my level of concern soaring. I am out of my league on what to do to help Chase and it's killing me.

Quickly, I shrug out of my plaid cotton button-down, leaving me in just a white T-shirt. I fold the plaid fabric over once, twice. It's soft and feels like it might be nice and absorbent.

Placing the shirt to Chase's head wound, I try to stem the blood.

Talking to Chase seems like it may be a good idea. Haven't I seen that in movies?

"You must have hit the side window," I tell my still-unconscious brother. "I don't know how that happened since you had your seatbelt on. But, who knows?" I pause. "Oh, Chase…"

The silence as I trail off becomes deafening. I gotta keep talking now. So, I continue, "Help is on the way, bro. Hold tight. You have a lot to live for. Don't you dare give up now, okay?"

I hear sirens in the distance, their plaintive wails growing louder and louder. Someone must have called an ambulance, the police, whomever. Thank God. Crazy thing is I personally don't need any help. Physically, I'm more or less fine. A little shaken up, yes, but that's it.

But how can I be fine when Chase is so obviously not?

Sighing, I silently pray to God: *My brother's been through enough shit in his life, he doesn't deserve this. He's finally found happiness, God, so please let him live.*

Chase isn't waking up, or even moving, and suddenly, I feel a surge of anger, anger I thought I had under control. But this ire isn't directed at my brother, or even my mom, who is all too often the target. No, this anger is directed at God.

Closing my eyes, I hiss, "You know what? Fuck you, dude. If you can't help Chase, then what good are you?"

Shit, I am going to Hell, for sure, for that remark. But if getting God's attention in this blasphemous way saves my brother's life, I'll go to Hell willingly.

His life for my immortal soul seems like a fair trade.

Someone knocks on the window just then, scaring the living daylights out of me. I just about jump out of my hide, and then look to see who it is.

It's no one I know, but, damn, quite a crowd has gathered outside the car.

The guy who is knocking on the window, still — some middle-aged business dude with a basset-hound face — yells in, "Are you all right, son?"

His eyes go to Chase's limp form, and then to where I'm holding the plaid shirt to my brother's head. Instantly, the businessman's basset-hound face falls when he sees how heavily the shirt is soaked with blood.

"Can you open the door?" he gently prods. "Your friend there doesn't look so good."

No shit.

I whisper, "He's not just some friend, dude; he's my fucking brother."

"What?" the man outside the car says. "I can't hear you. Open the door, son. Okay?"

I wish he'd quit calling me son. He's not my father; my dad is dead.

Suddenly, I lose my shit. I start to shake and cry. The businessman tries to open the door on his own, but it's locked. Between gasps for breath, I hit the *unlock* button.

The ambulance arrives at the same time the man who's trying to help swings open the door. But paramedics rush over immediately and shoo him out of the way before he can help.

I close my eyes and tell God I'm sorry for cursing him out. And then, for the first time in a long time, I pray for real.

With all my heart and all my soul, I beg God to let Chase live.

An hour later, I am at the hospital, waiting in the appropriately named waiting room. It's empty, and I'm glad.

After we arrived at the hospital, Chase was admitted immediately. Me? I was taken to an open ER room to be checked over, and since I was fine, I was released.

And here I sit, in the empty waiting room, waiting for my mom to arrive to take me home. Not that I want to leave anytime soon. I plan to stick around as long as I can in case Chase wakes up.

I just wish I knew more. But they won't tell me anything.

One thing I did find out, though, I know exactly how Chase and I ended up in the accident. Listening to the paramedics on the way to the hospital, I overheard them saying that the lady who hit our car was some ninety-year-old who isn't even supposed to be out on the road. Apparently, her license was revoked two months ago, when old age had taken away sixty percent of her vision.

Like me, though, she walked away from the accident unharmed. She'll be fine, unlike Chase. He is nowhere near being fine.

Not that I have any real info to base that assumption on. I just know he was still bleeding and still not awake when we were wheeled in to the ER on stretchers. After that, Chase was taken to a different part of the hospital, leaving me in the dark as to his current condition.

Guess the staff is waiting for our mother to arrive to give out any updates. She's been called and is on her way.

I sigh and glance around the waiting room.

Since no one is around, I can finally let go. Placing my head in my hands, I let the tears fall. And fall they do. Although a few minutes into my crying jag, someone clears their throat.

Quickly, like, lightning-fast, I straighten and wipe my eyes. Just in time, too. When I look up there's a young nurse before me.

"Oh, hey," I say to the girl.

The nurse is cute and not a hell of a lot older than me. Maybe she's a candy-striper. She looks like she's on an errand, since in her hand is a plastic drawstring bag.

She toys with the tie for a few seconds, and then asks, "Are you Will Gartner?"

"Yes," I respond.

She hands me the bag. "These are your brother's clothes and belongings. He won't need them—"

My whole world drops out from beneath me.

"What..." I whisper.

I can't even go on. What does she mean Chase won't need his things?

"Oh, no," she says. "I didn't mean your brother won't need his belongings because he's gone, like, *gone*. Mr. Gartner is just going to be staying here at the hospital for a few days, that's all."

I can breathe again, and I slump down in the chair on a long exhale of air. "Jesus," I say to the candy-striper, "you just about gave me a coronary."

"I'm sorry. I should have mentioned that he was okay first."

"You think?" I mutter.

I'm not trying to be a dick. I'm just tired and worried and out of patience.

Embarrassed, the young girl's face turns beet red.

She starts to leave, but I stop her. "Hey, can I see Chase? You said he's going to be okay, but what's wrong with him?"

Glancing around, she says softly, "It's not really my place to tell you how he's doing. I could get into a lot of trouble."

Jeez, she must be a new employee, all hip to abiding by the rules and all. "Well, okay. Thanks, anyway," I say flatly.

"The doctor will be in to talk to you soon," she assures me. "Um, are there any parents on the way?"

"Our mom," I reply.

"Okay, well, I'm sure the doctor will want to speak with your mom as soon as she arrives."

The young girl leaves, blonde ponytail bouncing behind her. I sit for a minute before I start to search through the plastic bag she gave me, the bag with all of Chase's things.

I find most of the clothes are covered in blood, no surprise there; blue jeans, a T-shirt with some ancient band's name on it.

"This shirt must be from the seventies," I muse, smiling when I think of how Chase told me he found a bunch of our dad's old record albums up in Gram's attic this past summer.

"Must have found this old thing, too," I say as I place the T-shirt back in the bag.

Under all of Chase's clothes, I find his cell phone.

I take it out and power it on.

I know the hospital has contacted our mother, but they have no idea Chase is actually married. My brother has thus far only shared *that* information with me, which makes me feel kind of special.

Time to make a decision, kid—that's what Chase would say.

I know he would want me to notify Kay, like, immediately. His wife deserves to know what has happened to her husband, right?

Without another moment's hesitation, I scroll through the contacts. When I find Kay's number, I take a deep breath, and then I hit *call*.

TWENTY

Kay

'M outside of the church, laughing and talking with Missy when my cell buzzes. She and I have just made plans to go see a movie when Chase returns home, a double date—possibly this weekend—me, Chase, Missy, and Nick.

Wow, who would have ever dreamed such a plan would be possible? Not me. But I'm happy we're past, well, the past. It feels right and good to forgive and move on.

I glance down at the phone when it buzzes a second time. Chase's number lights up and I say to Missy, "It's Chase. I better get this. He's probably about to board his flight and is calling to give me an update."

"Sure, of course. We can talk more about everything later." Missy starts to walks away, waving good-bye as she heads to her newly repaired car parked a few spaces away. "Take care, Kay," she calls out over her shoulder.

"You too, Missy. Bye." I give a little wave, and then

turn away and answer the call coming in.

"Hey, Chase. What's up?" Before he can reply, and in a low, seductive voice, I add, "You better not be calling to tell me you missed your flight. I have big plans for you when you get home."

"Um, this isn't Chase," the voice on the other end quietly — and embarrassedly — informs me.

"Oh." *Shit.*

I know who the voice belongs to, even as Chase's brother says, "Uh, it's me, Will."

"Will…" I trail off.

I am perplexed as to why Will would be calling me from Chase's phone. I'm also appalled by what I just said to my new brother-in-law. Mentally, I am face-palming myself.

And then Will says, "Kay, I have some serious news. Chase and I were in a car accident," and I forget all about being embarrassed or appalled.

Oh, my God, is this even happening?

I forget every emotion and every feeling. I'm too busy trying to catch my breath, trying not to crumple to the ground.

Leaning against my car for some much-needed support, I whisper, "Chase…he can't be hurt. Oh, God, Will, is he okay? Please tell me he's all right."

My world is crumbling, and it's oddly reminiscent of another time in my life when my world was shattered — the day I lost the person closest to me at the time, my baby sister, Sarah.

I whisper her name, and Will says, "What? Who's Sarah?"

Will doesn't know… No, he wouldn't. He's aware that I lost a sister, but he doesn't know her name.

"Nothing," I say. "Chase is okay, right?"

Maybe if I say it again and again it'll make it true, and

not just some hopeful plea.

Maybe my crazy ploy works too, since, as I recite my make-it-real mantra in my head, Will says, "Yes, Chase is going to be okay."

But then there's a sigh of sadness, and I dread Will's next words. "What is it? I say.

"You should probably fly back out to Vegas if you can. Chase hit his head pretty hard. I don't know much, Kay, but I do know they're keeping him for observation."

"You're okay, right?" I say. I'm still kind of stunned. How could I not have asked that yet?

"Yes, I'm fine," Will replies.

I blow out a breath. I'm glad he is okay, but I'm still so worried for Chase. Head injury? That can't be good.

All I know is that I need to go to my husband. Forget about packing, forget about everything. "I'll be there as soon as I can," I tell Will.

"Good deal," he says, before we disconnect.

The next few hours are a blur.

I book a flight on my phone before I leave the parking lot, shaking my head as I ask the dead air, "This is just a nightmare, right?"

No, it's not. This is real.

And then I'm driving, driving. I'm calling Father Maridale, and crying as I say, "I have to go to Nevada. I'm so sorry. I need more time off. Chase is hurt. Oh, Father."

"Kay, calm down," Father Maridale replies. "Are you in your car right now?"

"Yes," I sob. "I'm driving to the airport."

I'm a mess, still. But Father Maridale talks to me. He gets me calmed down enough so I'm not a danger on the road, to myself or others.

"We don't need two accidents today," he says.

"No, no, we don't."

"Take a breath."

"Okay." I breathe in deeply.

"Take another."

I do.

"You're going to be all right," he tells me.

"I am."

"Be strong for Chase, okay?"

"Yes."

And then Father assures me, "We have everything covered at the school, Kay. Go to Chase; take all the time you need."

"Will you pray for him?" I ask.

"Always, Kay," he says. "Always."

Several hours later — the next morning, actually — I finally make it to the hospital where Chase is being treated.

Will has kept me abreast of all the developments since before my flight took off and since it has landed. In the taxi on the way here, I talked with him the whole way. He told me Chase woke up and they ran a bunch of tests. Will said Chase asked for me, and he told him I was on my way.

Things look good, but you never know.

I find Will in the waiting room, third floor, down the hall from Chase's room.

"Kay!" He jumps up, rushes over, and gives me a hug.

"I need this hug," I say as I try not to cry.

"He's going to be okay," Will assures me. His arms around me are a comforting reminder of his brother, the man I love.

"Do you want to see him?" he asks, stepping back.

Nodding and wiping at my eyes, I say, "Yes, of course."

But when we turn to go, Abby is blocking the exit of the waiting room. I don't know where she came from, but there she is, about to go all momma-bear on me. Her arms are folded, and she looks uncommonly stern.

"Chase is sleeping," she says, in a scolding kind of way. "You can see him later."

"Are you kidding me?" I respond. "I didn't fly fifteen hundred miles across the country to deal with this crap."

"Mom," Will pipes in, his voice hushed but firm. "Be cool."

Abby ignores Will and focuses on me. "Only family is allowed in to see Chase right now."

I am so close to blurting out that I *am* Chase's family, but Will beats me to the punch when he yells, "Kay is his *wife*, Mom. She has more right to see him than even we do."

Oh, crap. How does Will even know that Chase and I are married? Chase must've told him, which is fine, but this is not how I envisioned Chase's mom finding out that her son and I eloped a few weeks ago.

Well, I guess that ship has sailed.

"Is this true?" Abby whispers, her face falling.

So much for stern momma-bear, I think.

She's looking at me, waiting, so I give her an answer. "Yes, it's true."

She blows out a breath and reaches back, her hand grasping for a chair. "You and Chase are *married*?" Sitting down with a thud, she says, "When did this happen? How did I not know?" She turns to Will. "Were you there? How long have you known?"

"I only found out yesterday," Will replies. "Chase told me while we were at lunch. Right before…"

He trails off, and I try to get us back to what's more important at the moment.

"We can talk about all of this later," I state. "Right now, I want to see Chase."

Actually, I *need* to see Chase. I've missed him and ached for him. But knowing he's hurt and in pain increases my pull to him. Our bond is *that* strong.

Will says kindly, "Come on, Kay. I'll take you to him."

My eyes flutter briefly to Abby. I'm not looking for her approval, but I don't want more drama when Chase is released.

Her green eyes meet mine, sad, resigned. Her son got married without telling her. He didn't trust her enough to share. Abby knows she's made mistakes, but the extent of the damage she has wrought has never been as clear to her as it is right now.

I can't be cruel, though, so I offer my hand to her, and say, "Come on, we can all go see him together."

Abby doesn't take my hand; she makes no move to stand. "No," she says. "He's yours, Kay. This is the way it should be. Chase is a man, and you're his wife. He doesn't need his mom."

"I'm sure that's not true," I say.

"It is, though." Abby wipes at a single tear. "I lost him a long time ago. And I have no one to blame but myself."

I close my eyes. What can I say?

"Come on," Will says.

I open my eyes and nod.

And then we go to Chase.

TWENTY-ONE

Chase

M Y dreams are weird, with a past, a present, and a maybe-future. I mean, what else would this mean—me, Kay, and a little boy, riding in a car? There may be a little girl there, too, but I'm not sure.

Back to the little boy…maybe he is supposed to be Will in my dream. But why would Will still be a little kid, while I'm my current age?

Two more things: if the little boy is my kid brother then why are his eyes blue—like mine. Not green, like Will's. And why is his hair dark—like Kay's—not blond, not light-brown?

I don't have any answers, so I return to dreaming, only this time I dream of Kay. Shit, my dream is so vivid I swear I smell my girl—sweet, clean, pure. Kay tells me she's not so pure, but she is. She's the bright light to my dark soul. If she wasn't in my life, where would I be? I was slipping and falling before I met her. Only a month out of prison and set on reforming—that was me. But I was still so drawn to sin.

With Kay, for the first time in my life, I think I may make it. Sweet girl gives me purpose, and she gives me the strength to work through the things that have been holding me back.

"Chase." I hear her voice, almost as if she is right here at the hospital. *Crazy.*

"Kay," I reply, eyes closed tightly. "I wish you were really here."

A soft hand caresses my arm. "I *am* really here, Chase," she says.

"Why?"

"You were in an accident, baby." *Oh, that's right.* "Will called, and I flew out last night."

I open my eyes.

This is not a dream. *Thank fuck.*

Kay is here, next to my bed.

In my bed would be better, I think. And then I say exactly that.

Will, behind Kay, mutters, "Dude, even in the hospital." He shakes his head. "You are so oversexed."

I roll my eyes and think of about a hundred smartass comebacks. But now is not the time.

"Hey, I'll catch you in a few," Will continues as he heads to the door. "You two need some time alone."

"You don't have to go," I say at the same time as Kay.

We look at each other and smile.

"No," Will says, grinning. "I think you both could use some quiet time. Just keep it PG-13. Mom or the nurse could walk in at any time. Oh, and by the way, Chase, Mom knows you and Kay are married."

"Is that true?" My gaze goes to Kay.

"Yes," she replies.

"Did you—"

Will cuts me off, "No, I told Mom. She was giving Kay a hard time about coming back to your room."

Kay shrugs. "It's no big deal, Chase."

Will clears his throat, and asks, "Are you mad at me, bro? That I told Mom your secret."

"No," I reply.

And I'm not angry, not at all. Kay and I weren't planning on keeping our marriage a secret forever. Probably best if the news trickles out slowly like this.

"All right, I'm out of here," Will says on a loud exhale. "You kids behave now, okay?"

Kay and I laugh and agree to "behave."

When my brother is out the door, I turn to my wife. "Will, the voice of reason," I say, chuckling. "I really must have hit my head, like, *hard*."

"Speaking of which…" Kay frowns and scoots her chair closer to the bed. She touches the bandage covering the stitches on the side of my head. "How are you feeling?"

"Eh," I murmur, "so-so. Better, I have to say, now that you're here."

Kay shakes her head, and she looks so damn stricken. "God, you gave me such a scare, Chase Gartner."

I reach for her hand. "Do you really think I'd leave you a widow this early in the game? We're only just getting started, remember?"

"God, Chase." She closes her eyes and winces. "Don't even say words like *widow*. A life without you wouldn't be worth living."

"Hey…" I squeeze her hand. "Open your eyes and look at me."

When Kay's soft caramels find my eyes, I continue. "Don't say that. If something were to happen to me, I'd want you to go on."

In a voice choked on emotion, she whispers, "I really don't think I could."

"You'd have to, Kay," I insist.

She shakes her head. "No. I swear I wouldn't want to."

"Hey, hey." I try a different way of convincing her. "What if it wasn't just you? What if there was a child to live for?"

We've had this talk before, but nothing has ever been one hundred-percent decided. Having this brush with mortality, though, has made me more determined than ever to create a child with the woman I love.

I just hope she's on the same page.

"Have you thought about it?" I tentatively ask.

She knows what I mean, and she replies, "Of course I've thought about it."

I can't discern where her thoughts lie, so I say, "If you're not ready, Kay—"

"No, I'm ready."

My eyes hold hers. "You're sure? Like, you're for sure, for sure ready."

That earns me a smile from her, as well as a tiny laugh, and then a mock-chastising, "Chase."

But then, more seriously, she adds, "I've thought about it a lot. And, at first, after we originally talked about having a baby, I did have some reservations."

"Oh?"

I must sound miffed, as Kay quickly amends, "Not about you, Chase. My reservations were about myself."

"You have to be kidding me. You'd make the best mom and you know it."

"Maybe," she says, her tone doubtful.

And then she tells me her fears.

I understand how her past has shaped her view of herself, but still, I reassure her, "You're going to be a great mother, babe. You can't keep thinking about the past. We've been through this."

Kay is mostly healed, but she still sometimes doubts

herself because of the Sarah-thing.

But she sounds more certain of her abilities to parent when she says, "I know, Chase. I just slip sometimes, though." And then she adds, "You're going to be the best parent, though. Our child will be lucky to be loved by you."

Kay is always telling me I love with my whole heart, my whole being, and maybe that's true. I do love completely, like how I love my brother…and how I love Kay. Thing is, my girl loves fully and completely, too.

"Come here." I tug her hand, urging her to come closer, even though I'm mired in tubes and wires.

Kay helps me shift that shit aside, and then she's right there with me on the hospital bed, lying by my side.

I turn my head and lean down until my lips meet hers.

And then I kiss her.

With our lips touching, she murmurs, "I don't want to hurt you, Chase, with all the tubes and stuff."

The thought of her hurting me is so laughable that I find myself pulling back and chuckling.

"Hurt me?" I can't stop laughing. "How in the world could you ever hurt me?"

"You know…" She touches a tube running to my arm. "What if I knock something out?"

"You won't." I pull her back to me. "And even if you did, I'll survive." As I brush my lips back and forth over hers, I whisper, "No more talking, okay?"

"Uh-huh."

She complies, and I kiss her. Her lips part, opening for me, and I touch my tongue to hers. Kay lets out a little moan and goes lax in my arms.

I'm suddenly hard as fuck, and I want her like nobody's business. "Lift up your dress," I command.

Kay leans back, and I take the opportunity to trail kisses down her neck, until I have her rasping, "Okay. Let me take my panties off."

I never stop kissing her, even as she lifts her dress to slip her panties down her legs. My lips travel down to her cleavage, kissing the neckline of her dress. And then I reach up and pop open a few buttons, exposing her lacy bra.

Kay is practically panting as she moves to straddle me, and I push up the stupid, fucking hospital gown I'm wearing and give her the tip of my cock. "Unh..." she moans.

She's always incoherent at times like these, and I have to smile, pleased at my effect on her.

"Ease down on me, baby girl." Arching my hips, I make it simple for her to impale herself on my dick.

And she does, with no hesitation.

"Fuck," I utter when we're fully joined. "You are so fucking wet. You must like hospital sex."

"I like *you*, Chase Gartner," she says.

She circles her hips, and then moves up and down my shaft slowly and lazily. It's all gentle and easy, at first. But then we start fucking—hard and dirty, and a little nasty. After all, what we're doing is forbidden and we could easily get caught, which makes it all the better.

Kay's hands are on my chest, and my hands are in her hair. The bed's making an awful racket, as is Kay, which compels me to whisper, "Shh, babe. Someone's gonna hear us."

"I don't care," she tells me. "Just keep doing what you're doing, Chase. Fuck me as hard as you can."

Her cursing, which is rare unless we're in bed, makes me start to come. "Shit," I groan. I prolong as long as I can, stilling inside of her, but my release is past the point of no return.

Kay starts to pulse around me as I come.

We are still panting, recovering, when, to my surprise,

I realize I am still rock-hard.

"Want to go again?" I ask, raising a brow and thrusting up into her.

"Yes, but" — Kay glances at the door — "what if someone comes in."

I laugh. "You weren't worried about someone coming in before." A strategic shift of my hips, cock still buried deep inside, makes her look like she's reconsidering.

"Still want to stop?" I ask.

"No, no way."

"That's my girl."

And it's true. Kay will *always* be my girl.

TWENTY-TWO

Kay

MESSING around in Chase's hospital bed is like playing with fire. And we find ourselves almost burnt. Luckily, though, I hear the voices outside the door before anyone ventures in.

"We need to make sure we're decent," I whisper to Chase. "There's someone in the hall."

But Chase is not done with me.

He thrusts upward, hard. "Not yet," he rasps, just before his hot mouth descends to one exposed breast.

"Uh, I don't—" Another forceful thrust, and I'm panting a different tune. "Oh, my God, I changed my mind. Don't stop, don't stop."

"Wasn't planning on it," Chase rasps.

When he feels my release, he lets himself go, and not more than a minute later, the door swings open.

"Close call," I murmur as I'm adjusting my dress and jumping back over to the chair next to Chase's bed with a speed I didn't know I possessed.

"Sheesh," I say, out of breath and still straightening my clothes. "We were almost caught red-handed."

Chase adjusts the sheet on his bed and whispers over to me, "That's what made it even more fun, right?"

I can't argue that point, so I just smile.

A lady in a white lab coat, the doctor, walks over to the bed. She's busy looking down at a clipboard, so I assume she's seen nothing. Chase's mom and Will are right behind her.

But just then, when I think our secret will never be discovered, I notice my pink panties sticking out from under the sheet covering Chase. *Oh, no!*

"How are we feeling today, Mr. Gartner?" the doctor asks, smiling kindly.

Thank God she's focused on Chase and not me, because I can't stop staring at the rogue panties.

Chase, unaware of my oversight in getting dressed, replies to the doctor, "Great, I feel really good. I think I'm ready to get out of here."

"Well, let's check you over and then I'll make a final decision on releasing you."

The doctor sends me an accusatory glance as she moves closer to Chase, and I'm fairly certain she's figured out that we just had sex. After all, she is a doctor, right? She probably knows the signs to look for, like my flushed face, or Chase's sly smile.

Crap, I hope it doesn't smell like sex in here. And then there are those damn pink panties. Talk about a dead giveaway.

When the doctor glances back down at her clipboard, I attract Chase's attention by nodding to the incriminating evidence of our lust gone wild. He chuckles when he sees the article of clothing I'm referring to. And then, to my relief, he covertly tucks the evidence farther under the sheet, all without the doctor noticing a thing.

Abby, though, sees Chase's actions and frowns accordingly.

Will, the ever-observant little shit, barks out a laugh.

"Great," I mutter under my breath. I know then that four of the five people in the room have now seen those damn panties.

The doctor looks up from her clipboard and gets down to business, focusing on her patient. After checking Chase's vital signs, she examines his head wound. With the bandage off, the stitches are in full view, and I wince at how painful they appear. There's a jagged line of black threads along the side of Chase's head.

Covered, his injury didn't seem so bad, not as real. But I can't deny the icy stab of reality that comes over me when I see how badly he's been hurt. It's a grim reminder that Chase could have been ended up a lot worse than this.

Reaching over, I grab his hand and mouth, "I love you,"

"I love you, too," he replies, his eyes searching mine. "You okay?"

"Yeah."

Part of Chase's silky, light-brown hair has been shaved off. When he sees me staring and staring, he chuckles and says, "Guess I'll be getting this evened up and going back to a prison buzz cut for a while."

"Guess so," I say. *But I'm sure you'll still look hot*, I think to myself.

Abby and Will continue to hang back, observing everything quietly.

While the doctor is writing notes on her clipboard, Chase asks her, "So, what's the verdict, doc? Am I good to go?"

"Actually, yes," she replies, glancing up. "I'm discharging you today."

With his eyes moving to me, Chase asks, "Any travel restrictions?"

The doctor shakes her head. "No, no restrictions at all. But I want you to follow-up with your family physician when you return to Ohio. And, of course, anything unusual that pops up, like sudden-onset headaches, blurred vision, that sort of thing, I want you to head straight to the ER."

"Yes, ma'am," Chase replies with a mock-salute and a smile that delivers.

The doctor blushes at Chase's charming ways.

"Anyway," she says, smiling back at Chase. "A nurse will be in with instructions for your aftercare. I think if all goes well, you should be right as rain from here on out."

"Not that he was all that right beforehand," Will mutters.

He's teasing, but Abby quickly chastises him. "Will!"

Chase laughs and says, "Relax, Mom." Turning to his brother, he adds. "And you—just wait till I'm back to one-hundred percent. We'll see who's 'right,' then. Or more likely, who is *left* upright."

"Bring it on, bro," Will shoots back as he pretends to flex.

Abby rolls her eyes, but like how I feel, there is relief and happiness in her expression. She's glad Chase and Will are both okay and able to joke around. I know this because the alternative is unthinkable...for both her and me.

The doctor leaves, and Chase and I get down to the business of discussing when we should head back to Ohio.

"You should stay a while longer," Abby breaks in. "Greg will be back tomorrow. I'd like to make a special dinner so we can all celebrate."

"Celebrate what?" Chase wants to know.

"That you and Will are okay, for one. And"—her gaze flits from Chase's face to mine—"we should also celebrate that you two are now married."

I know this is Abby's way of saying she's accepted our marriage, even though we chose an unorthodox route.

"So, it's decided?" Abby prompts.

"I don't know, Mom," Chase says. "I kind of just wanted to go home, you know?"

"Yeah," Abby replies, eyes downcast, "I know you need to get back."

But when Will pipes in with, "Please, dude, what's one more day?" I know we'll be staying through the weekend. Not that I mind.

Chase sighs. "You okay with that, Kay," he asks as he turns to me.

"Of course," I reply.

I'm fine with whatever is decided, since truthfully, I'm just thankful Chase is all right.

TWENTY-THREE

Chase

D INNER with the family on my last night in Vegas goes much better than the first dinner we sat down to, shortly after Kay and I arrived in town. The positivity in the air gives me peace, peace that everything might turn out okay with *all* of us. We're a little crazy, yeah, but we are still family.

Greg is his usual reserved self at the table, but there is genuine concern in his voice when he brings up the accident.

"You're a very lucky young man," he says to me just as my mom sets a pot roast in the center of the dining room table.

Turning to Will, he adds, "And so are you, son."

Normally my brother would shoot off his mouth about how Greg is not his father and don't be calling him son, that sort of thing, but today he just smiles and says, "Thanks, Greg. And don't I know it. Chase and I were both really lucky."

I think my near-miss with mortality has shaken Will. That, coupled with the quality time I've spent trying to reach him, and Cassie being out of the picture, leads me to believe that my brother won't be turning back to drugs to solve his problems. He knows there's nothing good to be found down that forlorn path. If anything, in our family, indulging our weaknesses leads only to disaster.

Once my mom is seated at the table, we dig into the delicious meal she's made.

After a few minutes of everyone enjoying their food, she asks me, "So, are you flying back to Ohio, or are you still planning on driving your father's old bike back."

"I don't know," I reply, glancing over at my new wife, seated next to me, for her take on the situation. "What do you want to do, Kay?"

I'd originally hoped to drive the bike back to Harmony Creek with Kay. But my thinking it might be nice to see the country seems like a poor idea now. Too much has happened, and the delays have messed with our work commitments.

"Well," Kay replies, frowning. "I'd love to drive back, especially on the bike, but I should probably get back to school as soon as possible. Father Maridale has had to cover for me a lot lately. I don't want to take advantage of his generosity."

"Yeah, I know." I blow out a breath. "I need to get back to work, too."

Abby nods. "Okay. Do you want me to ship the bike to Harmony Creek, then?"

"Uh…" I glance over at Will, who is pushing around peas on his plate.

Shit, I can tell the kid wants the old Indian to stay. He's done really well with learning to drive it, and in less than a year he'll be sixteen. Do I really need a motorcycle in

Ohio? Probably not. I mean, sure, I'd love to have the bike since it was Dad's, but Will has as much claim to it as I do.

With my eyes on my brother, I say, "Nah, why don't we just keep the bike here and give it to Will next summer."

Will's head shoots up. "Really?" he says.

Kay shoots me a smile and mouths, "That's sweet of you."

Mom shrugs and says, "It's your call, Chase."

Fuck, that hit on the head Friday must've really scared her. She's not turning this decision into a debate or a challenge to her authority.

But I want to be fair, so, as a group, we decide the Indian will stay. Even Greg agrees.

After dinner, Kay and I book our flights back home for the following day. I can tell my mom really wants to watch a movie—as a family—so I decide to give her this. Greg will never take the place of my father, but there's no point in shunning all activity involving him. After all, the family dinner went well enough.

Shit, I guess I *am* evolving.

But in one area I remain uncivilized. And that's when it comes to sex.

When I finally get Kay in bed—following two long movies and too much popcorn—I order her to lose the sleep shorts and tee immediately. "Get naked, sweet girl," I command when she emerges from the bathroom. "I want to taste how sweet you are."

Giggling, she starts to undress. But when she's too slow for my liking, I go to her and pretty much tear her fucking shorts right the hell off. I make quick work of the only thing I'm wearing, as well—my boxer briefs.

I'm hard as fuck, my cock throbbing, but I want this time not to be as rushed.

Back on the bed, I deliver slow, wet kisses across Kay's chest then up along her neck, making her murmur, "Oh, yes, Chase. That feels so nice."

She is already half-gone, even before I move up to her mouth. Parting her lips, I touch my tongue to hers. I know she loves to be kissed like this, all slow and soft. When I reach down and dip a finger into her slick folds, I use my thumb to work her nub.

Faster and faster, her breaths come. "Come for me," I rasp in her ear as I press my body to hers.

But Kay is intent on something more before she lets herself go completely.

"I want you inside me first," she whispers. "I want to come around your cock, Chase."

"Fuck, Kay."

She only talks like this in bed, and it never fails to make my dick even harder. With what I have to give her, I part her legs and settle between her creamy, soft thighs. Handling my cock, I rub the tip over her clit again and again. Her juices coat me and my hand, and then I can't hold back any longer. Plunging into my girl, I bury myself to the hilt.

Kay holds onto my shoulders as she tries to keep up with my ever-quickening pace. She moves with me, but when I fuck her really, really hard, she can't keep up.

Placing my arms under her knees, I hoist her up and say, "Let go, baby. Just enjoy it."

And, oh, does she enjoy it.

Following our releases, I lower her legs and settle my spent body gently on top of her. Our faces are inches apart, and I lean down to kiss her, murmuring, "I love you so fucking much, Kay. Where would I be without you?"

I shudder at the thought, and she wraps her arms around me. "Don't, Chase," she says. "No more worrying about what-ifs and where-would-I-be if you weren't around. I'm here, Chase. I'm in this for the long haul."

"Yes, you are."

I nuzzle into her neck, and she squeezes me with all she's got. I just give thanks, over and over again. I thank Kay for standing by me, for staying with me through all my stumbles, for picking me up after all my falls.

"You're a good woman, Kay," I tell her, my heart on my sleeve.

"And you, Chase, are a good man."

For the first time, I finally feel like maybe I really am a good man.

Yeah, maybe I am.

TWENTY-FOUR

Kay

B ACK in Harmony Creek, life returns to normal. I resume teaching my energetic class of eager-to-learn first-graders, and Chase returns to work too, fixing that which needs fixing.

It's also true that Chase and I are more in love than ever.

One warm, sunny late-September afternoon, following the end of the school day, I search out my gorgeous man. When I find him outside the rectory, repairing a loose shutter on a first-floor window, sans shirt *oh, my*! I take a few minutes to admire his hot bod.

I swear I will never tire of checking out Chase Gartner.

"Damn," I say, and then loudly enough to get his attention I let out a wolf-whistle.

Chase spins around, muscles flexing. "Didn't know you knew how to do that," he says, referring to my loud cat call.

"Ha," I reply, ambling up to him. "There are lots of things I know how to do, maybe a few you don't even know about."

I wink, and he laughs. "Oh, now I'm intrigued."

I add with a coy smile, "If we weren't on church grounds right now, Chase Gartner, oh, the things I'd do to you…"

I trail off and he takes a step toward me, slow and sauntering, with his low-hung jeans, chest bare, broad, and hard. My, he looks good.

Only inches from me, he stop and prompts, "Do continue, sweet girl." His hand goes to my jaw then down my neck like a whisper, where he stops and toys with the thin strap on my floral printed dress. "What would you do to me if we weren't on church grounds, Kay?"

His husky voice and searing blue eyes leave my panties dampened. "Chase…"

"Tell me," he insists. Leaning closer, he nuzzles the sensitive skin near my ear.

Gasping, I blurt out, "I'd drop to my knees and show you what I'd do if we weren't here at the church."

Chase groans, "Fuck, we need to get out of here, babe. Like, right away."

One thing I've noticed since we've returned from Las Vegas is that Chase's sex drive has hit full throttle. Pretty impressive since he's highly sexed as it is. Not that I'm complaining. Hell, no! And now is no exception.

I heartily agree. "Let's go."

No surprise, we don't even make it to the farmhouse. Mere miles down the road from the church and I am leaning down, undoing Chase's jeans, and taking him in my mouth.

"Fuck," he utters when I really get going.

There are advantages to living in the middle of nowhere, such as lonely, rarely traveled country roads.

The one we're on is not busy, but still, it's a main route. So, we turn off to a *really* empty road, and Chase parks off to the side. I crawl astride him, and he pushes my panties aside so he can thrust up into me.

Hard and fast, that's how Chase likes to fuck today. And wow, do I love it. I love it even more when his hands slide down into my pushed-aside underwear, cupping and squeezing my ass.

Pushing me farther down onto him, I am filled with his length, and together, under a canopy of changing leaves, we find ecstasy as one.

Afterward, spent and a little sweaty, I place my moist forehead on his shoulder. "Oh, my God," I breathe out. "I don't think I can even speak."

And then, true to my statement, I fall silent.

Chase leans down and kisses my cheek. "Was it that good for you, baby?" he asks, half-teasing, half-serious.

I am fully serious when I breathlessly reply, "Hell, yeah. And when, tell me, is it ever not fantastic?"

Chase chuckles, his chest, still bare, rumbling beneath me.

We both grow quiet until Chase says softly, "It's the end of September, Kay."

His words are not just words, they are filled with meaning.

I lean back and look at him squarely. "Yes, I know."

He presses his lips together, and I know he's about to say something serious.

"What?" I inquire. "What's up?"

In the softest, sweetest tone, one that just about melts my heart, he tells me, "I just hope we make a baby soon. I love you so much, Kay, and I can't think of anything else lately."

"I want that, too," I tell him, my soul as bared as his.

"It can happen now, right?" he asks, like he's making

sure.

"Well, I never got a new Depo shot, so there's a high chance of conceiving from here on out." Smiling and touching his jaw, I add, "Especially with all the sex we've been having lately."

Chase shifts beneath me. He's still inside me, never having completely gone soft.

He hardens more fully, and quirking a brow, I say, "Again?"

"Fuck," Chase laughs. "Do you even need to ask?"

He moves and I breathlessly murmur, "Guess not."

The next weekend, it's time to finally get around to the double-date with Missy and Nick. Chase is a little reluctant at first, but I talk him into it.

"It's not going to feel weird?" he asks, a reference to my dating history with Nick and his sexual history with Missy.

I am truly past all of that stuff, though, and I tell Chase as much.

He replies, "Okay, let's do it, then. Give them a call."

I do exactly that, and on Saturday night Chase, Nick, Missy, and I find ourselves all watching a movie at the newly renovated theater in town. It's a comedy, a good one, and we all laugh and have a great time. Afterward, we decide to head down the street for a late-night bite at the diner.

"To where it all began," Missy teases, nudging me with her shoulder as we walk.

"And what a great beginning," Chase chimes in when he overhears Missy's comment.

I smile at him as we continue on our way.

A beat passes, and, out of the blue, Nick asks Chase, "So, how's work going at the church?"

"It's good," Chase replies quietly.

"You must have most everything up to speed, by now, I'm guessing," Nick adds.

"Pretty much," Chase replies.

It's true: work has slowed down quite a bit for Chase at Holy Trinity. He's fixed most everything that needed fixing, and there's only been minor maintenance stuff to keep up with lately.

"You ever think of starting something on your own?" Nick inquires.

Chase shrugs and says, "I've thought about it, sure."

"So, what's stopping you?" Nick wants to know. "You can pretty much do anything. I'd bet you'd have so many jobs you wouldn't not what to do."

"Thanks, man," Chase says, laughing. "I don't know, though. I could handle the workload, but I just don't know all that much about the business side of things, you know?"

"A partner might be able to handle that sort of stuff," Nick suggests, his voice implying that this is more than just small talk.

Slowing to a stop outside the diner entrance, Chase turns to Nick. Missy smiles over at her boyfriend and nods.

"Ask him," she prompts as she and I stand by our men.

"Okay, what's going on?" I chime in.

Nick is a good guy, and I get the sense he wants to help Chase in some way. If he has a business proposal, I know it'll be something worthwhile.

Turns out, Nick does indeed have a proposal.

"If you were interested in starting your own contracting company," he begins, speaking mostly to Chase, but including me and Missy in the conversation, as well, "I'd certainly be willing to invest."

"Oh," Chase replies contemplatively. I can tell he's interested. "How would something like that work?"

"You'd have all the control," Nick assures him. "It'd be your company, really. Like a sole proprietorship. I'd just come in as an investor. We could work out whatever terms feel right to both of us."

Standing outside, under the glow from a nearby streetlight, Chase turns to me. "What do you think, babe?"

I can see in Chase's blues that he wants to do this. It is a good opportunity, no doubt, as Nick knows business from his years of running the pizza shop. This could be Chase's chance to create a future for us...and for our future children.

"I think it's a great idea," I reply.

"Then I think we should do it," Chase says.

And that is how Nick and Chase reach an agreement to go into business together — outside the diner where my relationship with Chase first started, where two broken people found a love that made them whole.

Sometimes things really do go full circle, one beginning leading into another.

And so it goes...

TWENTY-FIVE

Chase

I SET up my new business with Nick Mercurio — my unlikely, but somehow great-fit business partner.

"Fucking crazy," I murmur when all the paperwork is complete.

The whole time, though, I am smiling like crazy. I mean, shit, my own business. Wow! Who would've thought this former felon could turn his life around to this extent?

I would have never dreamed of such good things. But the true credit lies with one person. And it's not me. It's Kay.

She doesn't like to hear it. She believes I would've succeeded with or without her, but she couldn't be more wrong. She is my rock, my balance. Kay is golden, and if I hadn't already married her, I'd do it all over again today.

Speaking of which…

Following my late-afternoon business meeting with Nick and our new business attorney, I return to the farmhouse. I find Kay on the back porch, lazily swinging to and fro.

I take a seat beside her and give her a peck on the cheek. "Hey," I say.

"Hey," she replies, reaching over to take my hand. "How'd it go with Nick?"

"Great." I sit up a little straighter and proudly proclaim, "You are now looking at the president of Gartner Contracting."

Her arms fly around me as she tells me, "This is so incredible, Chase."

"It is," I agree, and pulling back so I can see her, I add, "Now that everything is coming together, we should talk with Father Maridale about that church wedding."

"You're right," she says. "His not knowing we're already married is starting to feel weird."

"Nobody in Harmony Creek knows," I remind her.

"Uh…" She looks away.

"Kay?" I prompt.

She glances over at me sheepishly. "I may have mentioned something to Missy this past weekend."

I'm kind of surprised Kay told Missy our secret, but I have no room to talk since I divulged the same info to my brother back in Vegas.

But does any of that really matter?

The way I see it, now that some time has passed there's no reason to keep our Vegas marriage a secret for much longer.

I relay this exact line of thinking to Kay, and she says, "True, but I think we should still talk with Father Maridale first. He'd be upset if he heard the news from someone other than one of us."

I agree, and the next morning, bright and early, we speak with Father Maridale. We find him in his office in the rectory. He's not mad or upset when he hears our news, but he is rather surprised.

"Oh, okay," he says, looking a little dejected.

He sure perks up, however, when we tell him we still want to have a church wedding at Holy Trinity.

"That's wonderful!" he says, glowing. I swear there are tears in his eyes. Kay and I tell him that we don't want to wait too long, and we all conclude a December wedding would work out best.

December is only two months away, but we plan to keep things small and intimate. I don't foresee planning on such short notice to pose a problem.

"You sure you don't want something big and fancy?" I ask Kay, just to be sure.

"No way," she assures me. "I like our plan just fine."

I feel the same way. I'm glad our nuptials will reflect our relationship—a relationship defined by a pure and simple love.

TWENTY-SIX

Kay

D ECEMBER rolls around and with it comes the wedding. I'm beyond happy. Well, happy except for one thing — I'm still not pregnant.

"Be patient, Kay," Missy says to me consolingly the morning of the ceremony.

She is in the church with me, helping me into a beautiful ivory lace wedding gown. We have the anteroom all to ourselves. "It will happen," she adds confidently.

"Easy for you to say," I reply, Motioning to her not-quite-so-flat belly, I lament, "You're already three months along."

Yep, that's right, Nick knocked up Missy…again. Only this time, it was planned. They were hoping for a baby to help ease the pain from the loss of their first one. And their prayers were answered.

In the meantime, despite tons of sex, I am still waiting for a single missed period.

"Don't worry," Missy assures me. "You'll be seeing that little plus sign on the stick soon enough."

"I hope you're right," I reply with a sigh.

Twenty minutes later, I am making my way down the center aisle of the church. The interior of the chapel is beautiful, aglow in soft candlelight. Among the modest gathering of guests in attendance are the ones who matter the most to me and Chase — Will, Abby, Greg, and my parents. Missy is my Maid of Honor. And Nick is Chase's Best Man.

The four of us, now bound by friendship, convene at the altar before a smiling Father Maridale.

"We are gathered here today…" Father begins, and I can't help but smile and smile and smile.

God, I am happy.

This isn't the first marriage ceremony for Chase and me, but already this one feels much more real than the one in Vegas. Don't get me wrong — that one will forever be special in its own right. But this one is amazing, surrounded as we are by our loved ones in our hometown. Who knew this would feel so incredibly special?

Not to mention, Chase in a superbly fitted black tux is all kinds of hot.

I squeeze his hand and venture a glance up at him from under my veil. He winks at me and sends me a soul-touching smile.

All I can think is: *I love this man.*

After the ceremony, a reception is held at the diner. Management was more than happy to oblige us when we first asked. They closed early and decorated the place just for us.

I have a plain napkin saved from one of the first lunches with Chase, and I hurriedly snag a pretty maroon one. This one, inscribed in gold, reads:

Chase and Kay
December 7

My husband catches me slipping my souvenir from our wedding day into my clutch, and he asks, "What are you up to, Kay?"

He drapes his arm around my shoulders and when he leans in close, I breathe in all that is Chase Gartner—a little soap, a little trouble, and a lot of virile male.

"Nothing," I reply. "I'm up to nothing at all."

I *am* up to something, though—a surprise for my beloved. The napkin I slipped into my clutch—as well as the plain white one I saved from the summer—is an integral part to my plan. If all turns out the way I'm hoping, I know it will be amazing to see Chase's face when I gift him with this surprise. But the timing will have to be right. In any case, I don't want to blow it now.

No need for me to worry. Chase is too busy whispering sweet nothings in my ear, which is rather distracting. With his warm breaths tickling enticingly at my skin, I whisper back, "Let's get out of here soon."

Our families, who are all staying at the farmhouse, pitched in and bought us a suite at the only hotel in town. We intend to christen it with our love tonight.

Plans are placed on hold, however, when Will saunters over.

"Hey," he begins, "what are you two crazy lovebirds up to?" Mock-punching Chase's arm, he adds, "You're not planning on cutting out early at your own reception, are you?"

"Actually—" Chase begins.

I quickly interject, "No, no, not at all. We're staying."

Chase groans, and I remind him, "We'll be alone soon enough."

"True," he murmurs under his breath.

Will, never one to miss a thing, laughs. "Good to see nothing has changed with you two," he says.

We head back over to our bridal table, which is just a large booth—the very same one Chase and I used to eat lunch at during our early diner days. Missy is on one side, seated next to her younger cousin, a girl about Will's age named Emma. Emma is pretty and perky, and her eyes light up when she looks up and notices a very good-looking Will heading to her table.

"Bro," Chase says in a low voice to his brother. "I think you have an admirer."

"Yeah! Wedding hook-up." Will pumps his fist. "Cool."

"Hey"—I smack his arm—"that's Missy's cousin. No funny stuff."

Will is a heartbreaker, just like Chase. Well, like Chase used to be. Oh, Chase is as gorgeous and hot as ever, don't get me wrong, but he's not breaking any hearts these days. He's all mine.

Will and Emma can't stop sneaking peeks at one another. Oh, they think they're coy, but it's quite obvious. I'm happy, though, to see Will has moved on from Cassie. He's been playing the field, becoming quite the ladies' man, according to Chase. But he's a good kid.

"I'm just teasing around," Will says sheepishly at the exact second we reach the booth.

"Hi," Emma says, smiling brightly as she looks up at Chase's brother.

"Hey," Will replies all nonchalant.

I shake my head. "He's just too cool," I whisper to Chase.

He rolls his eyes.

Meanwhile, Missy introduces Emma to Will.

She then slips out of the booth, and says, "I'm going to go find Nick. Emma, why don't you stay here and talk with Will for a while."

"Sure," Emma replies.

"Cool," Will agrees, his nonchalance faltering.

"Guess we're the designated chaperones," I murmur to Chase.

He laughs as we all clamber into the booth with Emma. "Guess so."

We all talk for a while and conversation flows easily. After some discussion of the ceremony and how good the food is at the reception, Will tells Emma about his plans for college.

"I want to go into graphic design," he says, watching this girl he's obviously smitten with for her reaction.

"That sounds very interesting," she replies. "Do you have any experience in that sort of stuff?"

"Actually," Will says proudly, "I do have experience, lots of experience, in fact."

I glance over at Chase as Will starts to detail his comic book projects to Emma. I don't think I've ever seen Chase as contented as when he watches his younger brother—this new, got-my-shit-together Will.

Will's issues were close to destroying him just a few months ago, but with Chase's determination and commitment to never again let his brother down, he has managed to save Will. And by saving Will, Chase has found an inner peace of his own, an inner peace that transcends the peace he's found with his father, and the peace he's working at with his mom.

Chase places his hand over mine. "What's this feel like to you?" he asks.

Will and Emma are now engrossed in their own conversation, so I am able to focus solely on Chase.

He seems so serious, so I ask, "What do you mean?"

His blue eyes, twinkling in the glow of the festive lighting, meet mine. "I mean"—he waves his hand around—"just everything. What's this feel like to you?"

I look around. My parents are laughing and talking with Abby and Greg, Missy and Nick are dancing, and all the other guests are enjoying themselves—eating, talking, having fun.

"It feels like a fresh start for all of us," I say to Chase.

He nods, and replies, "Yeah, it sure does, babe. We're starting a whole new chapter in our lives today."

I couldn't have said it any better than that, so I just smile and nod.

And that is the point where we fully turn the page on our old lives.

TWENTY-SEVEN

Chase

A T our wedding in December, I told Kay we were embarking on a whole new chapter of our lives. And these past couple of months we've done exactly that.

Life is still good—better than ever, in fact—when Valentine's Day rolls around.

The only hiccup is that Kay is *still* not pregnant.

Everything else in our lives is stellar, though. My contracting business with Nick has taken off, and even with the bad weather—it's been an exceptionally snowy winter thus far—I have more jobs than I know what to do with. I'm thinking I'll probably have to hire someone to help out by the time spring rolls around.

Me, supervising employees. Hell, Jack Gartner would be proud.

Other things in my life are good, too. I hear from

Will often. In fact, just yesterday he called to tell me he's planning on coming out to Ohio this summer. He stayed on after our wedding and spent Christmas break with us. It was a great time.

Anyway, I'm thinking since my brother will have his driver's license by the summer, he can drive out here if he wants. He'll have two options, too—drive the car from Mom (that fancy Challenger I discovered in the garage out in Vegas *is* for his birthday, just as I suspected), or he can drive Dad's old Indian motorcycle across the country.

It may be good for Will. Mom says it's up to him, and I'm cool with whatever is decided. Will is a responsible kid nowadays.

Crazy, I know. But it's true. The little shit that used to cause me so much grief now gets good grades, takes extra art classes in high school for college credit, and doesn't party at all anymore. He tells me his crazy days are behind him, and I believe him. Will left that shit in the past, along with the memories of his ex-girlfriend.

I can't be sure of how much contact Will still has with Cassie, but I know it's limited. They must see each other at school from time to time, I assume. Still, last time Will said anything about Cassie it was to tell me she'd gone into rehab last month.

Well, that's a good thing. I hope she can get her shit together like my brother has done. She's not a bad girl; she's just not right for Will.

Sitting in my truck at a stoplight in downtown Harmony Creek, I realize I'm utterly and completely lost in my thoughts when someone behind me beeps to alert me the light has turned green.

"Okay, okay," I mumble under my breath as I get my truck moving. "I'm going."

I drive another block then hang a right at the flower shop. Today is Valentine's Day and I have to take care of my girl. She loves flowers, so I plan to pick up two dozen red roses.

Ten minutes later, with my task complete, I head home to the farmhouse.

It's starting to get dark, even though it's only a little after six. Damn short winter days. In any case, Kay should be home from school by now. I wouldn't be surprised to find her in the kitchen, making me a special dinner.

When she first asked me what I wanted for Valentine's Day, I said, "Kay, you don't have to get me anything. Your love is more than enough."

However, I knew she'd want to do something special for me. So, when she pressed I told her I'd be happy with my favorite dinner—beef stew. Nothing like meat and potatoes—made with love—on a cold winter's day.

Well, whatever happens today, I've already decided I'm taking Kay out for a nice, fancy candlelight dinner tomorrow night. It won't be as busy since the day after Valentine's Day never is. And, besides, we'll both be more alert after a restful Friday night sleep with no work the next day.

Speaking of sleep, Kay's been so tired this past week. I hope she's not coming down with anything.

When I return home, sure enough, Kay has dinner waiting for me. And an hour later I am pushing my chair back from the dining room table, having finished a wonderful Valentine's Day meal.

"That was delicious," I tell Kay with a smile.

She smiles back at me from across the table. "I'm glad you liked it, Chase."

Kay's still smiling—not to mention she's been kind of quiet throughout dinner—so I know she must have something more planned, some sort of a surprise beyond the dinner.

"What are you up to?" I ask. "I know something more

is on the agenda."

"You got that right," she says, chuckling as she stands. Beckoning for me to follow, she adds, "Come on, Chase; come and get your real Valentine's Day surprise."

As she leads me to the hall and up the stairs, I assume Kay is taking me to the bedroom for some early-evening Valentine's Day sex. And, with that thought in mind, when we reach the landing at the top of the stairs, I spin her to me, lean down, and kiss her with all I've got.

"Mmm," she mutters against my lips when I slow things down. "What was that for?"

"Well, not that I need a reason," I reply, leaning back, "but you are looking rather hot right now. I couldn't resist."

Kay laughs. "Chase." She shakes her head, but her eyes are filled with love.

Kay is wearing a little red dress, and I skim my hands over her full breasts, stopping briefly to ply her sensitive nipples through the soft, velvety material.

"Mmm…" She leans into me, breathless already even though my hands are resting at her hips now.

"Come," I tell her, nudging her toward the bedroom.

But she stops me. "I want to be with you, Chase. I do, but not yet." I raise a brow, and she says, "I have something I want to show you first."

I stop groping my wife—for now. "Now you have me curious as hell," I confess.

With her hand on my chest, she pats me once and says, "Good. But you don't have to wait any longer to see this surprise. Come on, let's go to our room."

She turns and we walk toward our bedroom, while I am still wondering what this woman is up to.

At the door, she stops again and insists I close my eyes.

"Okay, okay," I say as I comply.

With my eyes closed, I allow Kay to lead me across the

threshold.

She stops when we're partway in the bedroom and whispers, "Okay, you can open your eyes now."

I do exactly that and, as I look around, I mouth, "Wow, amazing."

I am amazed, too. Our room is lit by soft candlelight and it's absolutely beautiful. But there's more...

At least a dozen red balloons are floating around the room. Some are stuck to the ceiling, their shiny ribbons dangling to the floor, shimmering in the glow of all the candles. And others are just drifting by.

Assuming the festive-looking room in and of itself is my surprise, I say to Kay, "This is really cool. I like it." I step around the dangling ribbons, touching a few balloons as I go. "It definitely looks like Valentine's Day with all the red."

Kay says softly, "I chose red balloons for another reason, Chase."

I give her a small smile. "Because of the one from the fair?"

She nods. "Yes."

I told Kay a long time ago about the red balloon my parents once bought for me at a fair when I was a kid. I thought that balloon was special, that it symbolized hope. But after they gave it to me, I let it go.

In a way, I lost my hope that day.

Kay tried once before to give me my hope back, at the church carnival last summer. But boy, did I fuck it up by not telling her beforehand what had happened between me and Missy. That night, when Kay heard me and Missy arguing at the bake sale booth, she learned the truth.

And that day, she let *her* hope go.

But now, we have all our lost hope back. These balloons symbolize not only my hope, but Kay's, as well.

"We'll never again let go of our hope," I say fervently,

turning to her.

"Never," she agrees. She touches my arm and adds, "That's not all, though. There's more, Chase."

"More?" I eye her questioningly. "What? There's more to my surprise?"

"Yes."

Kay pulls down one of the red balloons and hands it to me. I can see there's something in it, and I ask, "Napkins?" as I raise a brow.

She hands me a straight pin. "Pop it and see. It's part of the rest of your surprise."

I thought the balloons drifting around the room were cool, but if each one holds something, some memento from our past. Well, hell, that's even better.

I pop the first balloon and pull out two napkins. The first is a maroon napkin from our wedding reception at the diner. "Nice," I say as I turn it in my hands. "Now I know why you were placing it in your clutch."

"Yep, now you know."

The second napkin turns out to be a plain one from the diner, and I stare down at it, confused.

"It's from one of our first lunches," Kay explains, touching my arm. "I saved it and packed it away a long time ago. I wanted to have a reminder of our very first days together."

"I love it," I tell Kay, rubbing at the worn edges of the plain napkin, and then the smooth newness of the maroon one. "I'm glad you saved both."

"This way," she says quietly, "we can always look back. These are our memories, Chase."

"So" — I look up and gesture to all the remaining balloons — "each and every one is filled with a memory?"

"Memories, yes," she replies, looking a little sly. "And...well, more."

"Hmm," I reply. "This is very creative, babe."

She shrugs. "Well, since I can't do art like you, I had to think of another way to express my creative side. I wanted to make your surprise artistic in some way, especially since you're so artistic and I knew you'd appreciate the gesture."

I'm touched, and I tell her, "That's sweet of you, babe." And then I ask, "So, what kind of art is this, then?"

I'm curious to find out how Kay views what she's created.

"It's conceptual," she tells me. "The things inside each balloon represent our past. Well, except for one." She smiles, and says, "One represents our future."

Hmm, I wonder what she could have in the balloon representing our future. But I soon find out I have to go through the past ones first.

Kay hands me another balloon. "Pop it," she says, smiling.

I do as she asks.

Pop!

This balloon holds a wrapper from a wedge of brie.

I laugh.

Another balloon… *Pop!*

This one holds a tiny piece of baguette.

Taking a bite, I utter, "Delicious."

The balloon-popping continues, and I'm rewarded with more surprises.

Pop!

There's a tiny metal Eiffel Tower.

Pop!

I find oil pastels in the next balloon. I hold one of the colorful sticks up and say, "Hey, I needed these colors."

"I know," Kay replies, nudging me. "That's why I picked those particular ones."

"Aha."

Pop!

I find the scorecard from when we went mini-golfing last June, when I really got Kay going with my innuendo-laden words.

"I almost jumped you that night," she tells me.

"Shit, really?" I raise a brow, and she nods. "You should have," I add.

Sweet girl laughs. "Yeah, maybe, Chase, maybe I should have. But it kind of worked out okay, right?"

"It sure did."

Pop!

Ticket stubs from the drive-in movie we went to with Will and Cassie.

And then, a few more pops, and a few more mementos from our past.

When I reach for the final balloon, I eye it curiously. This is the last balloon, so it must be the one holding something representative of our future.

Huh. I just can't figure out why it looks the way it does, unlike any of the others I've popped thus far.

"Uh, Kay," I begin. "I hate to spoil anything, but I think this balloon is defective."

"It's not defective, Chase. Just look more closely."

I do as she asks. "Babe, there's a little balloon inside the big balloon. Is it supposed to be like that?"

Kay steps in front of me and lowers the doubled balloon so that it hovers between us.

"Yes, Chase," she says. "It's supposed to be like that." She takes the pin from my hand when I raise it up. "And you aren't supposed to pop *this* one."

"Okay," I say slowly. I am confused as hell as to what a balloon inside another balloon could possibly mean.

And then it hits me.

"Holy shit, Kay! Does this mean what I think it does?"

"Yes, Chase." Kay is looking at me with tears in her eyes, happy tears. "We're going to have a baby."

TWENTY-EIGHT

Kay

T is a beautiful October day, and I'm in the back of the farmhouse, rocking on the swing out on the porch. Missy is with me, leaning on the rail, and Chase and Nick are inside, talking business in the kitchen.

"Ugh, I'm as big as a house," I lament as I try to reach for a glass of water on the floorboards of the porch.

Missy leans down and helps me retrieve my water. "It won't be long now, Kay," she assures me, straightening. "You've hit the home stretch."

A baby cries from inside the house, and Missy is at the door in a heartbeat.

"That little girl has you and Nick wrapped around her finger," I say, laughing.

Before Missy has a chance to head inside to see what her four-month-old daughter wants, Nick calls out, "She's fine, Miss. I got her."

I take a drink of water, lower the glass, and say, "Nick

sure is good with the baby. Fatherhood suits him."

Sitting down next to me on the swing, Missy says, "Yeah, he is amazing. Chase is going to be a great dad, too. He's already so protective of you. I can't even imagine how crazy he'll be once the baby is born."

Rubbing my huge belly, I agree. "Chase will be a wonderful dad, I'm sure."

Missy peers down at my hand on my stomach. "By the way, I still can't believe you don't want to know the sex ahead of time."

"Chase and I agreed we want to be surprised," I tell Missy for about the hundredth time.

It's true. We don't have a preference. Boy or girl — as long as the baby is healthy we'll be happy.

Suddenly, as I'm feeling all maternal, a contraction hits. I've had a few false starts, but this one feels like it could be the real deal.

"Ow." I wince.

And then another hits…and another.

"Uh, Missy," I say nervously. "Can you get Chase for me?"

Missy has just been through this, and she jumps to her feet, a knowing look in her eyes. "Oh, my God, Kay, it's time, isn't it?"

"I think so," I reply.

Missy goes into full action-mode. "Chase," she yells into the kitchen. "Quick. You need to get out here, like, *now*! Your wife is in labor."

That sure gets his attention. Chase is out the door and on the porch in no time. My sweet husband, this is the first time I've ever seen him in a true panic.

"Jesus, Kay." He rakes his fingers through his hair. "What do we do first?"

"We should probably go to the hospital," I offer.

It's funny — for as panicked as Chase is, I am remarkably

calm.

"Yes, yes, good idea." Chase starts to help me up but then stops and reaches into his pockets.

"What's wrong?" I ask.

"My keys," he says. "Where are my keys? Shit, damn. I forgot where I put them."

Nick comes out with his baby girl, and he and Missy help calm Chase down. They help him find his keys, which are still on the table, and then we are ready to go.

Chase and I head to the truck, while Missy and Nick prepare to follow.

"I'll get her bag!" Missy calls out as she heads back into the house.

"We'll be right behind you," Nick adds, turning away as Chase helps me into the truck.

Chase and I don't reply since we're in too much of a frenzied hurry.

My husband does slow things down for a minute, though, as he takes the time to whisper, "I love you, Kay," before he buckles my seatbelt for me.

"I love you, too," I reply, just as another contraction hits.

"Shit," Chase says. "We better go."

"Yep, we better hurry," I agree.

Fifteen hours later, our son is born.

EPILOGUE

Chase
Six years later…

"D ADDY, I wanna thee a ga-raffe."
"You will see a giraffe, sweetheart," I reply to Sarah, my precious four-year-old girl. "There are a lot of giraffes at the zoo."

"Are there bears at the zoo too, Daddy?" my six-year-old son pipes in from the back seat.

"Yes, Jack. We'll see lots of bears there, too."

There has been a barrage of questions from my curious children since we left the farmhouse in Harmony Creek.

And these kids of mine are not done yet…

"Daddy, where's the zoo again?" little Jack asks.

"It's in Pittsburgh," I reply.

"Where ith Pithburg?" Sarah wants to know.

I laugh, and Kay twists in her seat to say to our children, "Jack, Sarah, please let your father drive in peace."

Her tone is scolding, yet gentle. We are such softies with the kids. Kay catches my eye as she twists to face forward, and I know she is thinking the same as me — we adore and love these two little blessings more than life itself.

A ruckus suddenly ensues over who gets to hold which stuffed animal and our sensible family sedan is filled with the sounds of screeching, indignant children for a good five minutes.

Kay gets them calmed down after a while and again settles back in the passenger seat.

"Just think, Chase," she says, grinning. "This is just the start of the drive. Jack and Sarah will probably get into a dozen more battles before we get to the zoo."

"I wouldn't have it any other way, babe." I tell her as I place my hand on her warm knee.

The summer sun shines in on her lightly tanned skin, just below the hem of her dress, and I think to myself: *This woman is so beautiful.*

Eyes back on the road, I smile and hit the gas to continue on our trek from Ohio to Pennsylvania. Ironically, the road we're on is the same path I traveled over a decade ago, and many times since.

But it's that long-ago June night that fills my thoughts today.

How different my life was back then. Fucked-up on a cocktail of drugs and seated next to my then-friend Tate, I had allowed myself to be poisoned by my past. I was bogged down in so much anger and resentment that I couldn't move forward.

The sedan cruises right over the spot where I was busted that night, the spot where my face hit the pavement. My actions that night led me to prison.

I usually feel sick to my stomach when I drive past this point, but today I feel nothing.

I have fully moved on.

I think again of Tate, the kid I was with that night. He's been dead for several years now. He never moved on, and the same shit that sent me to prison ended up killing him.

But my memories of him live on.

Tate used to like to say, "It's all about the numbers, man."

And I guess, in some ways, he was right—it is still all about the numbers.

It is one man, who once stood before one woman, seven years ago this month. It is numerous efforts—some failed, some successful—to get past everything, to reach zero judgments, zero doubts. It is eleven years after one big mistake, seven years after falling in love. It is two kids later. It's about two lives, who became four lives. All bound by one thing—love.

And that, my friends, is one pretty damn good life.

The End

Acknowledgements

First, so much gratitude and appreciation goes out to my family and friends who have supported me along this journey with Chase and Kay. The first grain of an idea for a story like this came to me along a back road in Ohio. In my mind, I envisioned a young man, lost, forlorn, a guy who's done bad things...but is good at heart. I always wanted the Judge Me Not series to be about finding redemption through love, and I hope I've accomplished that.

Next, as always, thank you to all the readers and fans of my novels. Without you, I'd have nothing but an unheard voice. Thank you for your continued support, especially to those of you who have stuck with Chase and Kay from the very beginning. Many thanks to the awesome team at Hot Tree Editing, as well. Your input and feedback on this final novel of the trilogy was invaluable. To Ari at Cover It! Designs and E.M. Tippett's formatting team, thank you. And finally, to everyone who works so hard to get my name and novels out to the world, thank you so much. Every time I see a post regarding my books on a blog—or anywhere in social media—I am humbled. Thank you to every single one of you. Your efforts are amazing. Additionally, a huge, heartfelt thanks goes out to my amazing street team—Team S.R. Grey. You ladies are more than a street team to me, you are my dream team.

Finally, love and thanks to Tom.

About the Author

S.R. Grey is an Amazon and Barnes & Noble Top 100 Bestselling author. She is the author of the popular Judge Me Not series, as well as the Inevitability duology and A Harbour Falls Mystery trilogy. Ms. Grey's novels have appeared on Amazon and Barnes & Noble bestseller lists in multiple categories, including #1 on the Barnes & Noble Nook Bestsellers list last year.

Ms. Grey resides in Pennsylvania. Her background is in business, but her true passion lies in writing. When not writing, Ms. Grey can be found reading, traveling, running, or cheering for her hometown sports teams.

Author Website:
srgrey.com

S.R. Grey Facebook:
www.facebook.com/pages/SR-Grey/361159217278943

Sign up for S.R. Grey's exclusive-content newsletter and never miss an update, cover reveal, or release:
mad.ly/signups/106801/join

Follow S.R. Grey on Twitter:
twitter.com/AuthorSRGrey

Find blog posts on the S.R. Grey Goodreads Author page:
www.goodreads.com/author/show/6433082.S_R_Grey

Follow S.R. Grey on Instagram:
instagram.com/authorsrgrey#

Read the first chapter of S.R. Grey's newest New Adult/ Romantic Suspense novel, Inevitable Detour...

CHAPTER ONE

I STARE at the computer screen. It's my last exam of spring semester, and there are only five questions left on the Strategic Management final before me.

My eyes are glued to words, forming a single question. I know the answer. Yes, I do. But then my vision blurs, and I think, *ugh, whose idea was it for me to major in business?*

Not mine.

The cursor on the screen blinks over answer choice B. Like I said, I know the correct answer, and it sure as hell isn't B.

What to do…what to do…

With a sly grin, I choose B and hit next.

I am feeling particularly defiant today. My parents left me a voice mail this morning, telling me in no uncertain terms that any thoughts of heading up to New York City this summer with my best friend and roommate, Haven Shaw, are best put to rest. So much for thinking it'd be fun to hang out in the Big Apple with Haven while she worked on finding an agent, making acting contacts, and generally just doing whatever it is a person needs to do when preparing to land a part in a play someday.

And not just any play.

"Broadway, here I come," Haven said the other day when we were discussing her big-city dreams.

She's a bit theatrical, but that's to be expected. She's a theater major, after all. Her goal is to eventually make it as an actress on the Great White Way.

Conversely, my dreams are much smaller. My primary longing lately is for something — *anything* — to happen in my mundane life. I thought New York would be a promising start. Guess not. Thanks to my parents and their aversion to anything fun for Essa, there will be no excitement in my life this summer. Nope. Just like the two previous summers, I'll be lulling away the time here at Oakwood College. Excitement for me will consist of chilling in the coffee shop on the edge of the tiny Pennsylvania town my small college is located in. My after-class afternoons will include exciting activities like staring out at cows and farmland, sipping on a mocha, and wishing and hoping for something more.

And that's just not right.

I'm a damn straight-A student, for God's sake. I don't need to spend the summer at Oakwood, taking stupid summer classes. Unfortunately, my parents don't care about my wants and needs. They believe their only child should apply herself year-round. Forget that I'm already a model daughter.

Well, more or less. But that's neither here nor there.

Bottom line is that my parents will not, as they put it in their terse message, have me "veering off course."

Oh, really? So they think…

My defiance hits full throttle, and I purposely choose the wrong answers for the next four questions.

I hit submit and think, *take that, Mr. and Mrs. Brant*.

Despite my actions, I'll still receive a solid A for the class. My GPA will not suffer in the slightest. Still, it feels kind of good to be bad.

That's sad, Essa, that choosing a few wrong answers on a final is the best defiant act you can come up with.

Sighing, I click a button to indicate I am finished with the exam. I then grab my purse from the back of the chair and head for the door. "You're pathetic," I mumble to myself as I step out into a warm, stuffy hallway that smells of varnish and books.

I kind of like the smell as it wraps around me. It's the smell of students seeking knowledge; it's the smell of youth. Despite all my protestations to the contrary, I do like college. I would just prefer to be studying something of my own choosing.

I stand and ponder. Not only does the smell of school envelope me, but the heat of the day does as well. The second-floor hall I'm lingering in is about ten degrees warmer than the classroom was. Dropping my purse to the floor, I shrug out of my olive-green mock-army jacket. I'm down to two layered tanks, blue over white, but I am still roasting.

"Blech," I pant, fanning myself as I bend down to pick up my purse. The button on my pants threatens to pop, and I let out a curse. I really should have worn a pair of nice, loose shorts instead of squeezing my ass into overly stylish skinny jeans this morning.

Maybe if the jeans were a little looser, I'd be more comfy.

I do a funny little dance in the thankfully empty area outside the classroom. Sadly, the jeans don't feel a single inch looser. Damn designers. Don't they realize we're not all model-perfect? When I exhale, the button squeezes once again at my middle, and I remind myself that I need to lay off the sweets.

Yeah, right. A girl has to have some kind of indulgence, right? And since I'm no exception, sugary treats are it for me. Otherwise, I'm fairly straight and narrow. I don't do drugs, and I don't smoke. I also barely drink—two drinks are my limit when I do imbibe—and I'm not promiscuous.

"Far from it," I mumble.

I've only had sex once, in fact. And what a disaster *that* turned out to be. The memory alone, from one of the few nights I deviated from my two-drinks policy, at a Saint Patrick's Day party two months ago, leaves me feeling nauseated. Yeah, the thirty seconds spent with the senior who was cowriting an article with me for the online *Oakwood College Gazette* just wasn't worth the time it took to take off my clothes. All too clearly, a fuzzy memory of him grunting on top of me, sweaty and harsh, comes to mind. I kept regretting that this was how I was losing my virginity. I still regret it. But what can you do? Last time I checked there were no time machines.

So, yeah, forget about sex. That's my motto. I'll stick with sugar-laden goodies for now. Like cupcakes. Haven made a batch to celebrate our surviving finals week. Her homemade buttercream frosting is far better than sex any day. Not to mention it's more orgasm-inducing than the thirty seconds that had me asking, "What? That's it? Why bother?"

I sigh. I need to get back to the apartment and hit up those awesome cupcakes. But my feet are far from moving. I can't believe I daydreamed away five whole minutes. Or maybe it's been ten.

Retrieving my phone from my purse, I send Haven a quick text: *Leaving Byers Hall. Don't eat all the cupcakes.*

A few seconds later, she texts back: *Oops. I got hungry and ate the rest for dinner. Sorry.*

Bitch, I reply.

Whore, is her response.

I call her a bitch again and laugh. She's laughing too. I'm sure of it. Haven knows my texts are sent with love. She is so not a bitch, and I would never think such a thing for real. Nor do I suspect she sees me as a whore. I am far from it, as established. Well, unless we're talking sugar. Then, I'm a full-blown slut.

Haven sends another text. *Just kidding, Es. I didn't eat all the cupcakes. I know you love them, so I left the rest for you.*

Aww, Haven is the best. *You're super sweet*, I text back, and then I start down the hallway. Finally.

As I amble along, I think of how Haven is definitely one of the better parts of my life. Throughout the course of the past three years, we've become best friends. We met at a freshman orientation. It was an early one, held during the spring prior to matriculation. We sat next to each other and clicked immediately, which is kind of amusing, since we're so different from one another. Somehow, though, we just work. Bottom line, I love Haven, and I'd do anything for her. She's certainly done some selfless things for me, no doubt about that. As a result, we're close, thicker than thieves some say. I tease Haven all the time; tell her she's my sister from another mother. Since her own mom passed away years ago, she usually replies that she'd let my mom adopt her. But then she adds the qualifier, "that is, if she wasn't so damn overbearing."

Understatement of the year.

Just the other day, after I received a call from my mom—she was checking in on my studying—Haven joked, "If your mom took me in she'd probably insist I change my major from theater to business."

"She probably would," I agreed.

It's true. My mother means well, as does my dad, but both my parents have a tendency to focus on practicality. And to the Mr. and Mrs. Brant, practicality means majoring in business.

"It's always smart to major in something marketable," Dad likes to say.

"Like business, honey," Mom always adds with a smile. "You're making smart choices, Essa."

Too bad they're not *my* choices.

Wishing I was more like Haven, who answers to no one, I round the corner and run smack dab into one of Haven's acting professors. To my dismay, it's the shitty professor who broke my friend's heart two weeks ago.

"Hi, Essa," Professor Walsh says cordially while pretending to step out of my path.

He remains in the way, of course. Still, I manage to slip around him. He nonetheless stays with me, turning and watching me the whole time.

Ugh. It is so hard not to snipe, "Get the hell out of my face, you fucking douche bag."

Since I lack the courage to say such a thing, I hold my tongue.

But when Professor Walsh reaches out and touches my arm, halting my progress, I twist from his grasp and snap, "Really?" I raise both brows and take a step back. "Please tell me you did not just lay your hand on me."

"Now, now," Douche Bag Walsh says in a sickly, patronizing tone. "There's no need for such a venomous retort. I don't know what Haven has told you —"

"Try everything," I interrupt.

Haven and her thirty-five-year-old professor had a three-month fling. It was all hot and heavy, not to mention illicit as hell, until he ended it in a not-so-nice way.

Concern fills the professor's light-brown eyes as he taps his foot and stares at me. It's not concern for the girl whose heart he's broken. It's purely concern for his own ass. Oh, the trouble he could get into for fucking one of his students.

"Don't worry," I say, just to get him to stop staring

celebrating the fact we survived our third year of college.

We did, didn't we?

Hell, yeah, I type back. *Seniors next year. Woohoo.*

I'll drink to that, Haven replies.

Me, too.

Hey, by the way, I hope you're planning on having more than two beers tonight. Rules are out the window.

Ha-ha. And, yes, rules are out the window.

Good, she texts. *Who knows, Essa, maybe you'll get so loosened up that you'll end up meeting your fantasy man.*

If only she knew it's her brother who stars in my fantasies. Just thinking about the man — and he is a man, not some fumbling college boy — gets me all worked up. But it's ridiculous to continue on like this. I'll surely never meet Farren, seeing as New York City is off the table.

Resigned to live my parent-directed life, which certainly does not include hot guys, I push all thoughts of my secret fantasy, Farren Shaw, to the back of my mind. Gathering up my purse, I stand. But before I leave, I think about the lecture I listened in on.

Fate…

Destiny…

What's in store for me? Where will these so-called predetermined events lead me? Somewhere, everywhere, nowhere. The possibilities are endless. Still, I have to wonder if there will ever be an inevitable detour in *my* life.

"Yeah, right," I quietly scoff. The only inevitability in my future is that my life will continue as planned. But the instructor's words resonate in my head, reminding me that we can't escape our destiny and that we always end up where we're supposed to be.

Of course, for that to happen, it may require a bit more defiance on my part. Particularly when it comes to my parents and where they expect me to spend this summer.

and, hopefully, go away. "Haven won't let me go to the disciplinary board, and God knows she'll never do it herself, so your secret is safe."

The professor, more confident as soon as he hears I plan to keep my mouth shut, lazily brushes back a lock of wispy, dirty-blond hair that's fallen to his forehead. He's boyishly handsome, and this is a move he's obviously perfected.

Too bad it does absolutely nothing for me.

Undeterred, he says in a low voice, "Everything that happened between me and Haven Shaw was consensual. She's twenty-two years old, Miss Brant. Last time I checked that makes her an adult."

I feel like screaming in his smug face. "You were her freaking professor, prick. Not only did you violate school policy, but you violated her when you let her fall in love with you and then callously walked away."

But there's no point in lashing out. Haven is still hung up on the guy, shady though he is. She doesn't want him to get into any trouble. And someone might hear me if I start going off in defense of my friend. The halls are empty, but many of the classrooms are full.

So I don't say a thing. I do, however, scowl at the man. And then I walk away, leaving him standing in the middle of the hall. I feel his eyes on me, probably checking out my ass. His hooking up with Haven wasn't some fluke. It's common knowledge that Professor Walsh has a thing for college-age girls. Until Haven, he was known as a one-and-done kind of guy. But he was really into Haven, for a while…until he wasn't.

It's really no surprise he liked her as much as he did in the early days of their fling. Men find Haven irresistible. And why wouldn't they? The girl is gorgeous. She is far prettier than I am. Haven is tall, with a model-like body. I am short, not super thin. Haven has big, expressive aquamarine eyes and shiny, raven-black hair. I have boring hair that can't even decide what color it wants to be. Some days it appears light brown, other days it's more of a dark blonde shade. Not that I pay much notice. I usually just pile the long, unruly tresses up in a sloppy bun, or twist the mess into a ponytail.

I'm not saying I'm unattractive. I just don't really stand out in a crowd. Not like Haven does.

Despite all she has going for her, Haven is far from conceited. She's unassuming and genuine, loyal to the core. That's why I maintain that she didn't deserve to be treated the way Professor Walsh treated her. He used her for sex, strung her along, and then unceremoniously dumped her with no explanation two weeks ago.

My ire at the jerk professor escalates. By the time I reach the stairs, I am smacking my hand down on the dark wood railing in anger. Quickly, I spin around, intent on stomping back and having one last word with the guy.

But he's long gone.

"Chickenshit," I murmur.

Sighing, I step over to a wall and lean back against it. There's a classroom a few feet away, in session. Leaning my head back, I listen to the soothing murmur of voices, thus allowing myself a few minutes to calm down.

Soon, I am relaxed. I also find I am fully engaged in listening to the lecture. Not surprising since the instructor, her voice light and feminine, is speaking on a subject I find fascinating—the role of fate in our lives. I walk over to the door and press my ear up against it.

"Wonderful," she says. "You've all shared some great insights. But now that we've dissected Shakespeare's use of fate in *Romeo and Juliet* and *Macbeth*, I have a question for you, a question regarding *your* lives."

The class titters, she chuckles, and I step back to where I'm able to lean against the wall. After a minute or two, I slide down to a seated position.

"What I want to know," the instructor continues, "is who here believes that real lives — *our* lives — are influenced by fate?"

"I do," I whisper. *At least I think I do.*

The professor calls on someone in the class, a girl. She responds, "I believe all of our lives are influenced by fate. And I firmly believe in destiny."

"Is there a difference?" the instructor questions.

The girl replies, "Yes, I think so. I've always heard that fate refers to the bad things that happen in our lives."

"And destiny?" the instructor prompts.

"It's the good stuff."

"That is a commonly accepted belief," the instructor concurs.

There's some shuffling of papers.

"What it all comes down to," the instructor continues, "is that every person's life is destined for a certain path. We may not realize it, especially when it's happening, but we *will* end up where we're supposed to be."

Wow. I think about my own life. I believe in concepts like fate and destiny. But, to my chagrin, I don't feel as if either has ever touched my life. In some ways, I suppose my parents have prevented *things* from happening by the way they've structured everything for me. Still, I hold out hope that something that is "meant to be" will eventually occur. If that doesn't happen, what will become of me? My biggest fear is that I'll graduate from college next year — with my shiny, new business degree — and move right back to my hometown of Philadelphia. Maybe I'll become an accountant, like my mom and dad. And maybe, like Mom and Dad, I'll never really *live*.

"Ugh." I place my face in my hands. I don't want to be an accountant. I'd rather eat pocket lint, I swear. If I had my way, I'd much rather work as a writer, a journalist of some sort. I find joy in writing articles for the school paper. But, really, if I dare to dream big, I see myself as an investigative journalist. The kind that seeks out exciting stories, stories with an element of danger.

Who in the hell am I kidding? I'm play-it-by the-rules Essa Brant. "Let's be real here," I whisper.

Sighing, I return my attention to the instructor and her big words on fate.

"Remember," she says. Her tone is so very serious, so very ominous. "Just because you think fate or destiny hasn't yet guided your life in some noticeable way doesn't mean it won't happen. I promise you, my friends, you will end up where you're supposed to be. And how can I say that with such certainty? The answer is simple: You can't escape your destiny."

Okay, so where will fate lead me? What is my destiny?

On a roll, the instructor goes on. "Things happen in our lives that are predetermined, whether we realize it or not. Often it's a series of small events that slowly and methodically lead us to where we're supposed to be. But sometimes it's a big, cataclysmic event that changes the course of everything. Even so, you may not realize your life is changing at the time. Something may happen to someone you know, perhaps someone close to you. Their 'something' ends up affecting you. *Your* life is now altered; *you're* set on a different path." The instructor pauses, and then she says, "Think of this path as an inevitable detour of sorts."

Everyone in the classroom is so quiet you'd hear a pin drop if someone were inclined to drop one. Guess everyone is deep in thought, wondering what "inevitable detour" is in store for them. And how will this "detour" alter their lives. God knows that's what I'm thinking.

"We have about ten minutes left," the instructor announces, breaking the trance she was holding everyone in, including me. "Are there any questions, class?"

A lively Q&A ensues, and I know it's high time I get up off my ass and go home. But I can't leave, not yet. I need a minute to take in all I've heard. It's like when someone puts something in your head, and that's all you think about. Now, I can't help but imagine an inevitable detour of my own. Maybe I should take charge and make one happen next week. I could defy my parents and go to New York City with Haven. It might be worth my parents' ire to finally venture out of the only state I've ever known. Not only would my bestie and I have a great time tearing up the town, but I'd be staying with Haven in her older brother's apartment. And there's a good chance that though Farren Shaw travels a lot for some crazy-secretive job he has, I'd finally have an opportunity to meet him. Possibly, I could even spend some time with him.

Gah. A thrill shoots through me at the thought of spending even a mere minute with Farren. Now there's an inevitable detour I'd like to take. Much like his sister, Farren is gorgeous. He has the same raven-black hair, same model-perfect features, like full lips and high cheekbones. His eyes, however, are not aquamarine. They're better; they're a unique and stunning shade of green. Not that I've had the pleasure of viewing these stunning green eyes in person. Only in pictures have I seen them, since, sadly, I've never actually met Farren. He's not around much. He was in the military for years, special ops according to Haven. And though he was discharged over a year ago, he still spends a good deal of time in other countries for his "work." Consequently, he's never visited Oakwood College campus. That's why I've never met him. And that is why I'm so incredibly upset about New York. That would have been my chance. Travel or no, he'd have to stop home at some point.

Oh well. Guess I'll have to continue to rely on pictures

and short videos of Haven's incredibly handsome brother to fuel my libido. And by fuel, I mean on all cylinders. I may not have much of an interest in sex, but I am still a woman. And, as a woman, I sense a man like Farren could change my mind on the sex-thing. He's like some dream guy — tall, dark, and too handsome for words.

So, yeah, I'm into him. It's mostly a secret, though. However, I must confess that once, several months ago, Haven caught me uploading pictures of Farren from her computer to my phone.

"Cyberstalking my brother, I see," she teased as she walked over to where I was seated — rather uneasily at that point — on the sofa in our living room, her laptop in my hands.

"No, no," I stammered while trying to close all the open windows…of Farren in uniform, Farren standing next to Haven, and Farren — a recent shot — in a finely tailored suit.

"He does look good in that one," she said, tapping the screen before the picture of her brother in a dark suit disappeared.

She was right. Farren in a business suit was all kinds of serious hot, so I had to agree. Then, I turned from the computer and asked, "Does he have to wear suits for his new job?"

She shrugged. "I don't know, Essa. I guess."

"What exactly *is* his new job?" I pressed. "You said he's some kind of personal security contractor, right? What does that mean, exactly?"

"I don't really know," Haven admitted. Then, with a laugh, she said, "All I know is whatever Farren does he gets paid a lot of money."

"I hope it's nothing illegal," I mumbled under my breath.

Hey, it's not so farfetched to think such a thing. Not

only does Farren fund his sister's college education—as well as all her expenses—but he also has plenty of money for himself. He owns some of the best real estate in the world, including a luxurious New York City apartment. The place is sweet, very sweet, located on the Upper West Side of Manhattan, in a high-rise building right next to Central Park. I've seen pictures, and it looks like the kind of place a celebrity would live in. Not that I care about the money Farren has, but the fact that he has so much of it does make me curious.

See, Farren and Haven Shaw were not born into any kind of money, not like the level of wealth Farren currently possesses. Their childhood circumstances were far from ideal and not anywhere near upscale. Their dad, a man named Alan Shaw, disappeared, seemingly into thin air, when they were very young. At the time, Farren was ten and Haven was only three. Their mom was left to struggle on her own to support her two young children. And she was doing okay, until she was killed in a car crash. Seventeen-year-old Farren and ten-year-old Haven were sent to live with their aunt—someone who absolutely did not want the burden of her sister's kids. Her aunt was cold and indifferent. Haven has said many times that her aunt was far from nice. That's why Farren joined the army the day he turned eighteen. He left and started sending Haven money right away. Their aunt was always cheap with them, buying the kids only the bare essentials. Despite all of those things, to this day, Haven still craves family. She tries so hard to maintain a relationship with her aunt. But the woman rarely—if ever—returns Haven's calls.

My phone vibrates, bringing me back to the present. It's another text from Haven.

Where are you? You better get your ass home soon. We're still going out tonight, right?

Of course, I type back. *I haven't forgotten that we're*

Good, okay. That's fine with me.

'Cause I think I'm finally ready to start pressing B every chance I get.